Author Bio

G ray Rankin has been teaching other people how to be creative for decades, but this is the first time he has published his own writing. He has worked in the UK and Europe.

He lives in the north-east of England, where he teaches, writes, takes photographs, swims, collects fossils and looks up at the stars when the clouds have parted. He enjoyed flying hang gliders and riding motorcycles for many years, and is the proud father of two exceptional human beings.

This collection features new and original science fiction stories, mostly about dystopian and post-apocalyptic worlds, with explorations of the human condition included at no extra charge.

www.grayrankin.com

Other Writing

You can read another short story of the author's, 'The Flit And Phil,' in 'Fragments – An Anthology.'

'It is a beautiful piece with fantastic attention to detail – it sits somewhere in between a prose poem and a dramatic monologue, revealing a story as well as painting a series of vivid pictures.'

– Dr Ann-Marie Einhaus, Associate Professor, Humanities Dept, Northumbria University, 2024

ISBN 9781861355065

Seven Tales Of Sacrifice

Gray Rankin

LitGo Press

First published by LitGo Press August 2024

Paperback ISBN 978-1-0687623-0-7

eBook ISBN 978-1-0687623-1-4

Hardback ISBN 978-1-0687623-2-1

THEMA category FLQ

BISAC 028070/029000

Book Cover by Graham Rankin

Dedication

To my Dad, who departed this world in 2023, and is no doubt still busy fixing things in the next, spirit level and try square in hand.

When you lost your voice, I found mine.

Let the saw do the work ...

Contents

Preface

After decades of teaching others how to write and develop stories, I have at long last found the time to put together a collection of my own. Better late than never, I hope!

I have used UK English spelling and grammar conventions in all the stories except for one. The last part of 'The 10:16 From Inai' finishes with scenes set in the US, so localised (or even localized) spellings seem more appropriate. In the first part of this story, I have based some words and descriptions on the Lakota people's lexicon, to recognise and honour the different ways it's possible to look up and interpret the stars.

I would like to sound a discreet word of caution about the story 'Shiny Head,' for anyone who has been affected by suicide, as there are brief references to it in the backstory of a family who encounter a time-travelling robot.

A sincere thank you for taking a look at this collection. If you would like any further information, you could head over to grayrankin.com. And if you enjoy it, please tell your friends and family, and feel free to leave a review wherever you think people will read it!

Gray Rankin
September 2024, UK

Speed Dating Checklist

W e are all busy these days, with our hectic schedules and fulfilling lives. And as a result, not a lot of time to find the ideal partner. But with the birth rate in such decline, the government has just introduced free speed dating sessions in many of the most popular meeting places. I intend to take full advantage of this today to secure a partner with clear reproductive potential. This could gain us the procreation bonus – a full year of extra credits – if we can successfully add to the population. The government is clearly desperate to do something about the crisis, and I fully support this bold initiative.

So here I am in my living room, all spruced up and ready to go, in a stylish shirt that was my last present from Mother. When she passed away, I inherited all the medical and diagnostic devices she had helped me learn to use. And fortunately, she also gave me the benefit of her wisdom, as a former doctor, with what to look for in a future partner – and what to avoid! Life just hasn't been the same since she went. It would be marvellous to have a woman around the place again.

Looking out of the front window, there is a landscape of apartment buildings, stretching as far as the eye can see until the heat haze turns the horizon into a shimmering blur. Ten years ago, when we moved in, there was a great view. But the daily temperature has risen considerably since then. Most walkways outdoors have been enclosed from the heat and the dust. If you don't use the blowers on the windows here every couple of days, you can't even see out.

I haven't seen the horizon from my window since I was left on my own. I presume the hills to the west still exist, but I'm not going on a trek outside to find out. You don't need to go out when can get everything you need delivered to your door, and I suppose I'm lucky that Mother made a small fortune from her private consultancy work, and the bank card she left me still functions.

Anyway, I have my positive mind locked in and am almost ready to set off. I know how to use the diagnostic gear I've inherited very well, and obviously I'll be taking most of it with me. Mother had let me practise with it to keep me busy when she needed her private time with clients and their special medical needs. And I have my checklist to go through with each prospective suitor, as I don't want to miss anything. It's my passport to procreation!

With so few viable partners around and so few chances to meet them, you can't afford to make a mistake. And there's so much to consider! Like life expectancy, and the calibre of any potential children, for example. That, after all, is the whole point. I can't risk combining my DNA with anyone else who's got some faulty coding in their genes. I have my certificates ready to show each date, and they'll have to show me theirs. The government is quite clear on that.

That's why thorough testing is such a good idea. All participants have signed a contract to allow a thorough examination, during the dating process, with approved devices. We all know it will happen. As a 100 percent healthy specimen, I expect no less of my future partner. I want top of the range progeny, so I am prepared to be rigorous in the selection process. Quality above all. And of course, the women can assess me too. They won't have the professional equipment that I do, but they are welcome to use whatever they can get their hands on.

We are, of course, not allowed to share the results of any testing with potential suitors, as we are not doctors, and the government is anxious not to encourage any false alarms or panicked demands on our health services, which barely function now in any case.

As I head down in the glass-sided escalator to the transport pods waiting below, I can't help remembering how exhilarating that was when we first arrived. You almost got vertigo trying to keep up with the changing height and the fast descent. Now you just dive headlong through clouds of brown dirt that hang in the air like a failing sky. The dust should have been soil in the fields, growing food crops so we don't have to eat all the bland processed stuff from cartons and packets. But farming outdoors here failed years ago, leaving only dust bowls where crops had once grown in fertile fields. Now the basements of the blocks grow extra food under artificial lighting, mostly watered and fertilised by all the residents. We try not to think about all that too much. You kind of get used to dulling your taste buds.

I enter a glacially chilled transport pod and give the destination. The driver makes comments about how rarely residents of this sector use it these days, but I don't feel like chatting, so I ask it to mute itself. My backpack, brimming with my portable testing equipment, is securely sat next to me on the bench seat.

I am looking forward to using it all again. I hope I get lots of positive responses! The odds, being a sprightly male, are of course in my favour, given the calamitous drop in fertility over the years for the rest of the population.

Some people say it's the artificial food we all eat. Some say it's the overly-warm climate. Others that it's pollution of one kind or another, silting up all our reproductive organs. Whatever the cause, I have my DNA certificate ready in case any females ask to see it. I had to send a sample to a government laboratory, to get it checked for viability. I am proud to say it came back with a double positive. Top quality seed, with tangle-free bidirectional genetic strands. Exactly what the lucky ladies will be lusting for, I joke with myself. And I will need to see their reproductive certificates too. They must, of course, have high reserves of healthy eggs and cycle through the months like clockwork, hopefully without a hint of headaches or hysterics.

Arriving at the centre, I heave my rucksack onto my shoulder, and stride in with a sense of heady expectation. I check in at the desk, and am directed to an upstairs hall. Taking the stairs, I am surprised with the extra effort my rucksack is taking to carry, so I pause halfway and pretend to admire the extravagantly airy open-space lobby, which extends upwards for several floors. All that heat and dust on the outside, and all this light and heavily filtered air on the inside. I know where I'd rather be today!

When I have made absolutely sure that I am not sweating under the armpits, I carry on, but at a more sedate pace. Being out of breath would clearly demonstrate a diminishing aerobic capacity, and my likely success at courtship would be scuppered from the start.

At the doorway to the hall I am registered, and then handed my ID pass, which I proudly sport around my neck for all to see. Participant B6, ready and reporting for duty! I like the way we are given numbers, as it keeps a comfort zone of anonymity between us all. If there are any promising matches, we can always swap names later, but the checking has to come first, of course.

In the old days, or so I've read, suitors would seek a certain spark, and want their heart to skip a beat! There's no time for all that now. No point being in love with someone who is infertile or prone to inferior offspring. The quest for the best DNA eclipses all that emotional turmoil.

The doors are opened for me, and I walk inside the hall, confidently enough but without projecting any hints of arrogance, I hope, as I consider my modesty a sizeable asset. Executing a swift eye sweep of the space, I try not to connect with anyone, and to give the impression of a man comfortable in new surroundings, with nothing to hide. There are tables of women around the sides. They all appear to be smiling in my direction, but I try not to smile back to any in particular, as I want to give all an equal chance, and avoid any subconscious favouritism. I begin to wonder if I am the only man there, but before I can discreetly scan around for any rivals, I am ushered to the first table, where Amazonian beauty A12 awaits.

We exchange certificates of overall and reproductive health, and everything seems in order. Reaching into my rucksack, I move the general scanner to one side and pull out the anomaloscope. It can test for tetrachromacy, and she looks at it with mesmerisingly gorgeous eyes of deepest emerald, which caught my attention straightaway. She sees four primary colours on the test, not the usual three, meaning she has true four-cone eyesight. Great for her, and useful no doubt for her career as a well-known artist, but sadly a negative result for me. I don't mind her having superior vision, and being able to see much more of the spectrum than me, but I've read that tetrachromatics too often produce colour-blind children. For me, the possibility of imperfection in sight for my progeny is too great. I can't roll out the red carpet if they might trip up on it. Sorry, A12, but you're not for me.

On to the next table, where A9 sits with her enticingly long legs, folded so expertly under the table they would make an origamist blush. She blinks slowly, drawing attention to her beguilingly sculpted eyelashes. First test results are promising, so I continue. Vision is fine this time, so after some pleasant anecdotes from her, about her career as a ballet dancer, I move on to cardio performance. This has lots of separate tests devoted to it. As she holds the pink ECG device on her chest, I look at the monitor on my wrist screen. There is a discernible murmur. She has a minor flutter. The irregularity is not serious at the moment, but it could deteriorate, or be a condition passed on, and I can't have that. She will have to find another ballerino. I thank her for her time and move on.

Next to the lady with the fluttering eyelashes and heart is A7, who looks like she has just stepped out of an advert for a Scandinavian holiday, when such things still existed. Clearly of Viking heritage, she has an aura of desirability that encompasses her very being. The hall lights reflect off her hair at certain angles, adding an intoxicatingly golden tinge to her Nordic locks. The tests I run all confirm her excellent physical condition, befitting her career as a fitness instructor. I smile with satisfaction, as does she.

Then I notice her shoulders. As I like strong-looking women, I may have let her appealingly muscular definition get the better of me. Just to be sure, I sweep my MRI wand over each shoulder. A good job I did. She has a rotator cuff tear on the left one and it is not healing straightforwardly. Even with specialised therapy, she will be in discomfort for some years yet, and may eventually require a risky operation. I need someone with two fully functioning arms from the get-go, and this isn't the sort of tenderness I was thinking of. No can do. She may have shoulder issues from her training at the gym, but it's quite a weight off mine to end this session.

Next up is A10. I assume that, as there is no pattern to the numbering, in relation to where the women are sitting, they have all been allocated tables at random. I recognise this one as an actress who has starred in several popular films I have watched. It appears the entertainment industry is as short of viable males as the rest of society. Money and success apparently aren't everything then, I reassure myself, and so perhaps fertility has levelled the playing field!

We get on well and she is impressed with my tip-top certificates. All is going well until the cardio monitoring intervenes again. She has a slight valve issue, or more precisely some mild aortic regurgitation, which could result in a weakened left ventricle eventually causing some kind of stroke. It is too much of a risk. Even if she produces quality offspring, she might not be around long enough to properly share the intensive child raising I have in mind, which might reduce my share of free time in the future. So it looks like she won't be co-starring in the movie I'm directing. Fortunately, there are some other prospects left.

Along to A11. We get along swimmingly, and I am beginning to relax and enjoy the experience of dating so much more now. I am breathing more easily, and notice I am making eye contact more naturally. We vault all the early hurdles with aplomb, and I feel that the low-dose x-ray test from my handheld scanner is just a formality. I can feel an inner glow of confidence begin to arise. Perhaps A11 is the one? She certainly has an engaging personality, and has devoted herself to nursing for many years. I slowly skim the scanner over her subtly sculpted cheeks, and on down to the base of her perfectly positioned chin, which shows no sign of under or overbite.

Regrettably, the x-rays do show a decay in her second bicuspid tooth in her left upper jaw. The decay has gone up into her gum. The screen flashes a warning. Upper gum decays can eventually spread south and lead to heart complications. Too risky. She should have had it seen to months ago. Probably too tired after all those night shifts caring for the sick to see a dentist. Wrong priority. The female form is clearly a very vulnerable thing, especially for some of these ladies. A slight smile of regret and apology, then I move on.

At the next table, A14 smiles alluringly, and confidently passes her certificates over for inspection. She has medium golden-brown hair, about a 5.3 according to the spectrophotometer readout, with a roughly 2b curl type I'd say, and it is arranged to fall fetchingly across the cheek that is angled a touch more forward towards me. As the tests effortlessly proceed, I learn she is a successful music teacher and has taken part in many concerts.

She has sensitive and dexterous-looking hands, with impeccable manicuring, and simple but elegant rings. I notice one of them seems to be made of copper, and her thumbs are just a touch arched out over, so a quick scan over her fingers is in order. As I suspected. The thumbs show hints of an eventual joint deformity, so an inflammatory disease may be on the cards for later life. Despite her current high level of competence in piano and keyboards, she might not be able to teach any of my brood for long enough to get them to the standard I expect them to attain. And her culinary skills may be affected too. I need someone who can feed a large family without a second thought. She's clearly struck a wrong note with her off-key thumbs, so no.

A13 starts promisingly, as usual I suppose, as some pre-selection has clearly taken place, and I must say the outward appearance of all the specimens so far has been very pleasing to the eye. She has rock-solid certificates and an interesting past as a former special forces soldier, with exceptional scores at sharpshooting and unarmed combat. If the security situation outside the blocks keeps deteriorating, she could be very useful to a young family.

I feel myself being drawn in to her delightfully tinted eyes, which have flickers of darker hazel around the edges. The amber highlights towards the centre dazzle as they are accentuated by the reflection of the light from my ophthalmoscope. Focusing in on the right one, I wait for the reading on my wrist screen. Disaster. Some of the blood vessels in the retina are leaking a slightly yellowish fluid. Although A13 doesn't know it yet, she is very likely in a pre-diabetes phase. And that might lead to a minefield of related complications later on. I shield the screen from her inquisitive gaze and mask my disappointment as best as I can.

"On reflection, I don't think it would work," I manage to say. "I'm a pacifist."

It is a lie, but she is so wonderfully deadly that I can't think of any other way to move on. I nod once, as if to acknowledge and empathise with her undoubted disappointment, and pick up the diagnostic gear. Such bad luck for both of us, A13, but it's over and out from me.

On to A8, a red-haired beauty with lightly sprinkled freckles and rich, oceanically blue eyes, a very rare and fetching combination, which must have really stood out in the courtrooms where she practiced law. She lets me analyse a blood sample with a diagnostic finger lancet, which indicates the MC1R gene, as expected, but the rare 0.17 percent chance of both red hair and blue eyes necessitates further tests. Everything checks out well, until I ask her to swallow a small pill and put on the DaTscan headset over the enchanting forest that is her hairline, so I can run a dopamine transporter check. Her eyes stare into mine, their hints of sapphire retaining a hold on me as I step backwards to await the results.

A few seconds later, my wrist screen flashes caution. Abnormal distribution of dopamine. To be sure, as I am finding her bewitching eyes hard to resist and would desperately like the negative reading to be false, I switch the headset to the vision tracking function, and record her eye movements as she responds to my prompts. As I feared. There are tracking errors suggesting cell loss. A nervous disorder is incoming. It could be years before it arrives, and we might be blissfully happy until then, but it is future time I cannot afford to sacrifice. Mistrial is my verdict. Case dismissed.

As I walk over to A15, my heart almost skips a beat. What a beauty! After complimenting her on such stunning looks, checking her certificates are in order, and running most of the preliminary tests, I decide that acquiring further data on a professional model will be fascinating, starting with a full comparative facial scan. This checks her measurements and proportions against the standard database. I run the instrument around her face and her profile gets a cracking 94.8 straightaway. It looks like she has an almost flawless forehead, not surprisingly perhaps as it gains a 91.2. I could spend all day looking at her exquisite nose, but the scan is far quicker and awards a 96.3 for the adorable outline. Her visage is finely rounded off by the smoothly flowing contours of her jaw, which merits an impressive 95.2.

The scan comes up trumps, as she scores an average ratio of over 94, putting her impressively in the top ninetieth percentile of available partners, as you'd expect from a woman who's made a living from the way she looks. And her complexion is so clear that her pores just ooze healthy genes and reproductive possibility. I am becoming enamoured.

Until, that is, I start the last test and move the diagnostic wand, which I've set to a multi-contrast MRI scan, up her sides. What may turn out to be the beginnings of an infiltrative disorder in the left kidney show up. Probably treatable. But not what I would want to have to deal with. So it's another no, sadly. She won't be featuring in my family photoshoots. The tests are being carried out for a reason!

After what seems like an all too short period of time, during which I have had exclusive access to a number of exceptional, yet sadly biologically flawed women, I move on to the last of the options for the afternoon. I take a deep breath and move across to A6.

She seems pleased to see me. And I her, for she is another stunner. Her certificates are as clean as a whistle, and she has a naturally classy air about her. I run all my checks and scans, and there is nothing untoward. I can scarcely believe it, so just to be sure I ask if she would mind me running through them once more. She replies of course not, and time seems to fly by as I do so. The results are just the same, and again I find nothing wrong with her. Quite the reverse. She is in excellent health, and is about as prime an example of the female form as you could wish to find. Her heart is pumping away like a precision instrument. She is surely the one.

She peruses my certificates with a smile, and they seem to please her. I ask her if she wants to run any tests on me and she replies no, she is more interested in character and the tests won't be necessary, as she wants to trust a partner to disclose any relevant conditions that they are already aware of. Otherwise, for the future, *qué será, será* is the order of the day for her. We discuss our thoughts on the ideal number of children to have and agree that three seems the best number. She says she would like to try to start a family as soon as possible, and I say that is my ambition also. She is from a very well-off background, and so hasn't needed to have a career as such, which suits me just fine. She confirms she is comfortable in a more traditional role in the family, and so at last I start to believe I have found the perfect match.

At the end of the allotted time I thank her and say I hope we will be able to meet again soon. She smiles and says she hopes so too. I relax and know that something special has just taken place. We have made a connection on every level. Out of all the possible partners I encountered, the best option was waiting right at the end. How Mother would have approved of this one!

We stand up together to say farewell for now. She offers me her left hand to shake. I am shocked and have to try hard not to flinch. I take the hand and shake it rather limply with my own left. If only I'd made it the first thing I'd looked into. It would have been so easy. So simple. But it wasn't even on the checklist. What an omission! How maddening.

Now everything is too complicated. She looks a little perturbed. She asks if anything is wrong. I say no, no, not to worry, I'll be in touch. She looks confused. I gather up my equipment while trying to appear relaxed, then turn away and sigh, relieved that I've only just avoided making a terrible mistake. I'm so lucky she shook hands – thank goodness for her upmarket social skills! Left-handers have a heightened risk of dementia in later life, I have learned, and are prone to more illnesses than usual. After a quick half-smile of goodbye, I turn away and realise I am not sure if I made a last eye-contact or not. Not to worry.

When I'm older, I want to enjoy seeing my children become high achieving adults, not have to devote my time to being in the corner full-time for some southpaw with softening synapses, no matter how wealthy. Dodging that blow was lucky for us both, as with the first sign of her lights going out I'd have thrown in the towel, and sent her away for someone else to have the bother with.

Avoiding the gazes of all the unquestionably disappointed ladies, I exit the hall and head on back to the desk set up outside.

"Thanks so much," I say to the ladies at the desk. "That was most enjoyable, and I've had a fabulous time. Unfortunately there's no one quite special enough at the moment."

The two ladies look at each other. They do not look sympathetic.

"I will happily attend your next session," I say reassuringly. "I'll be sure to find someone there!"

They look at each other again. One is frowning. She speaks.

"I'm afraid that won't be possible," she says in a rather cold voice. "There won't be any more sessions."

"But surely there are other women who want to get together with suitable partners and reproduce?" I suggest.

"No," the second woman says. "This is it. They are the last with childbearing potential. And there have been five men before you already, who left with their new partners. You are the last fertile people we have data on here. There is no one after you."

"Would you like to try again then?" the first woman asks, as if my response is just so predictable.

Apparently I have no choice. I mumble something about having a little time out, and go over to the large windowpane. It has a layer of fine dirt over most of it, but there is a clearer patch in the middle and I stare outwards, gathering my thoughts.

Things are much worse than I had been led to believe by the government. We are not just in population decline, we are at the end of the line. Just as Mother predicted, despite helping all her clients with fertility issues as best she could.

I owe Mother a better hope for the future. She must be able to see her grandchildren. It was her last wish to be preserved by cryogenic suspension, until I can deliver offspring, and she left me the finances to fulfil the contract she'd booked with a company to get herself frozen. Regrettably, I had to cancel the procedure at the last moment, due to my own need for resources and the difficulties leaving the apartment due to the climate catastrophe, and make alternative arrangements. As a result, she is now perfectly preserved in the freezer at home at considerably lower cost. Once her grandchildren were procured, I was going to contact the company again to enquire about the defrosting and regeneration procedure when they had perfected the process. I was so looking forward to introducing my future spouse to her.

I resolve to try again. It should only take a moment to rekindle the spark with the last suitor. I decide I might be able to overlook the left-handedness issue after all. And I could take a gamble on her going the distance in the rematch.

I go back to the ladies at the door.

"On second thoughts I might have been a bit harsh with some of them," I say, trying to sound assertive and in control of the situation again. "So, yes, I think I'd better have another look."

"Maybe," responds the first lady. "But remember that according to the contract you agreed to, it's now their turn to examine you."

I hesitate for a moment, and then nod.

They gesture towards the entrance to the hall, and somewhat sheepishly I make my way back in. I try not to look too defeated by circumstance, but this proves challenging. I catch a glimpse of A6 exiting by a rear door, which she deftly closes behind her with her left hand. On each table in front of the other suitors there are sets of testing equipment. No one is smiling.

The 10:16 From Inai

Hi out there! I am Kan-Ra, and as part of a science project I have to write a message to someone on another planet! Of course, we all know it's unlikely anyone will ever receive it, but we're young, and we can dream, can't we? So here we go.

Like me, you are probably living on a planet circling a double star system in the liveable zone. Apparently, most of the stars in the galaxy are doublers, so the chances are your planet is floating round a couple of them. We're lucky here because ours are quite similar in size and age, so they revolve regularly around each other.

Every time our planet, Inai, has revolved on its axis for forty-five spindays of spinlight and spindark, our suns will have completed circling around each other and everything starts again. Our scientists call this the Taku-Skani Cycle, but the rest of us just call it the sun dance!

You other double system dwellers will already know how orbiting two suns affects your life, but for anyone else out there on a planet in a single star system – yes, I know this is really unlikely but play along! – well, you probably have no idea how every last thing is affected, so I'll try to explain a bit more.

We have a kind of circular journey around our suns, Makai and Wakasai, because they are moving round each other smoothly and this pulls us around them in a regular orbit overall. But when the suns change positions, our planet is pulled inwards or outwards in an arcing radius, as if we were tracing round the edges of a giant eight-petalled flower. This is why we have named a real flower with eight petals the Inai Flower, and all offspring are encouraged to grow them in their gardens to help them understand how our system works.

Our complete journey around the suns takes three hundred and sixty spindays of our planet, during which there will have been eight full sun dances of Makai and Wakasai in the centre. The spindays can be mapped exactly onto the three hundred and sixty angles of the journey, as everything is locked together by attraction. It's lucky it all matches up, as we measure our lives by all these circles.

Every complete spinday we go through has a number, and that's how we count the orbit going by, and understand where we are in our system. Today is sixty-one, which means our suns have completed a full dance already, and are almost halfway through their second one. My existence day is on two hundred and seventy-one, just at the start of the seventh dance, so I have quite a while to wait before my family can celebrate. I have had sixteen existence days so far, so my age is sixteen orbits!

Everything on our planet depends on where the suns are on any given spinday. When they line up and one eclipses the other, it gets colder, spindark is longer and we have high tides. When our moon, Petai, also lines up with our suns in front of the planet, our tides are really high and there can be huge floods. This is why we build our dwellings near the coast on pillars to raise them off the ground, or burrow them into cliffs way higher than they need to be for the rest of the cycle.

For two separate quarters of each dance, both of our suns are in the sky, and we can see them track straight across it as Inai turns. This means spinlight is longer, and spindark is shorter, as one sun rises before the other. During these parts of the dance it is very hot, and we try not to be outside, as the double set of rays is too strong for our eyes and skin.

The territories in the central bands of our planet, the Okagai Lands, receive the strongest amounts of light, and are not lived in by us or by animals, as it gets too hot during spinlight and there is little or no rain. Some Inaians do travel across them during the rest of the dance when it is cooler, to have contact with those who live in the south. If we fly over them we have to be very careful not to do it when both suns are present, as the rays are even stronger higher up and we can get ill very quickly.

Across many, many orbits, my ancestors believed in The Beginning, a story about how our planet was made when Makai the mother sun and Wakasai the father sun merged together and produced Inai, our home, and all the other planets in our system, which they cared for in their space garden. Eventually it became time for Inai and the others to leave their parents, and the planets wandered across to their current positions. The love from both parents was still shown by every dance, when they swapped places to watch over us.

When we are younger, we go with our teachers to museums, which are full of specimens of the insects that live underground in the Okagai Lands. But we used to imagine that monsters lived there, and we'd frighten each other with tales of how they'd chase us until we got lost, and we had to hide and wait for the Kin-Rak to rescue us. We believed the Kin-Rak was a kind-hearted being sent by Makai and Wakasai to protect and save us.

As we discovered more truths about the Mahpiyai, the giant star ocean all around us, made up of all the suns and planets everywhere, we realised that our double sun system was made from the shrinking gas clouds produced after the Great Wakinai, the start of everything. But we still call our suns by their story names, because we say the journey of understanding is like flowing with the current downriver, and you can't change the name of the places you set out from.

Our scientists tell us that most star systems have two suns, and some have more. Many believe that the one-star systems used to have a partner sun, but it migrated away, leaving what we call a widowed star, or it was absorbed by the larger of the two, leaving what we call a cannibal star. In our region of space there are even systems with up to five stars! I can't imagine life there on a planet very easily. Five stars in the sky would be a great challenge to figure out. What sort of Taku-Skani Cycle could five stars have? Fortunately, two is the perfect number as everything makes sense if they are regular ones, like ours. We call them married stars.

All offspring learn about the reality of space at school, and there are songs about it to help us understand it better. We draw and paint our system when we are young, and we treasure these pictures as symbols of how our knowledge grows as we get older. I have included some drawings of mine when I was younger here, but of course I know these will never be seen by anyone else outside our system, because only the voice waves will travel if one day this is read out and sent into space! As we learn more, we have to be able to draw our whole system from memory, and include the right number of spindays and sun dances. Of course, we make our own existence day stand out from all the rest!

Because everything on Inai depends on where Makai and Wakasai are in relation to each other and us, every house has an orbit calendar on the wall. We need to know which spindays are going to have dangerous sunlight levels, so we can stay at home and do our learning indoors. It is the same for the southern Inaians, who live beyond the Okagai Lands, because as our axis is vertical we share the same climate. Of course, everything is upside down for them! We make jokes when we are young about how they have to tie themselves down so they don't fall off the bottom of the planet. I'm sure they say the same ones about us.

From our earliest days, we learn how to look up at the sky in spindark and find the patterns connecting the stars of the Mahpiyai. We group them into the faces of our famous scientists, like Dey-Itra, who discovered attraction and then explained how to measure it, and Het-Poki, who worked out that our inheritance trees come from prior species. Southern Inaians can see the faces of other scientists represented by the stars visible from their side.

In this way, our knowledge is all collected together and shared above our heads all round the planet. As Inai revolves around our suns, the stars change, and so do the scientists we all talk about as they come into view. As a species, we developed to understand our world and its connection to space, and grouping our stars into the faces of famous scientists helps us to explore and remember their ideas.

We have learned that there may be planets in other sun systems in the Mahpiyai where the axis is tilted, either because they formed that way, or a huge meteorite hit them. They could even have collided with another planet, when the system was forming. What a sight that would have been!

They say a tilted planet would have opposite climates, which would change as it went round on its orbit. This might restrict changes in the inheritance trees of animals because they would have to keep adjusting to warm and cold climates, or have to migrate over huge distances. For this reason, our scientists say advanced life is more likely on perpendicular planets than tilted ones. Even more odd, it's said that if a planet has a tilted axis, then its sun or suns would arc across the sky instead of tracking in straight lines like here on Inai. I can't imagine that at all. Shadows would be all over the place, and there wouldn't be a Path Story, which means so much to us as it guides our lives.

Because the dance of Makai and Wakasai takes place horizontally across the sky, we say that the boundaries of this path are like the boundaries of our lives. We must always move forward, learning new knowledge and helping others to develop theirs. We say once we are started on this journey, there is no way back to the kind of beliefs we had as young offspring.

The path also allows for us to be wrong, in which case we think of ourselves as having taken a bad turn, but we can get back on the right path by understanding why we were wrong, and apologising to anyone we have upset. There is no shame for us in being wrong, only in refusing to admit it. Everyone has the right to make mistakes, just as we did as a civilisation before we discovered real science.

There is also no shame in admitting that we didn't understand something. What would be the point in pretending to know something, when you didn't? Understanding when we have strayed from the path of knowledge, and when we need help, is so important that there are songs we learn about this when we are young. 'Everyone lives the Path Story, and everyone writes the Path Story,' as we say, and for encouragement all we need do is look up at the parallel tracks of our suns.

Science governs our lives, like the natural laws govern the star oceans and everything in them, and it is our life's purpose to explore these ideas in our own way, through telescopes, experiments, equations, and stories, for example. Our culture is rich in ways to understand our reality. Being a scientist is one of the most important roles in our society, and the best ones can spend their whole lives studying reality. They will be fed freely and cared for, as long as they share their knowledge, which of course they are only too happy to do, as ideas belong to everyone.

Although we say Makai and Wakasai are married stars, and of course a marriage between equals, we know there are differences in what they are made up of. We can see this in rainarcs when both suns are present in the sky. There are slight differences in the banding of their colours, so we know the composition of each one is not the same, just like Maken and Wakasen in real life, as we are named after our star's role.

I am a Wakasen, which means I carry around inside me reproduction equipment to fulfil my role. We can combine our fertility tubes with those of a Makai to produce a new offspring every orbit. These are hidden away safely inside the bodies of both genders so they can't be damaged by the special double spinlight times when both suns are sending their rays into our atmosphere.

Scientists, investigating Het-Poki's theories on prior species, have found evidence of the four-legged creatures that we came from in ancient rocks. They also had hidden fertility tubes, which must have passed down the inheritance trees and ended up in us.

Although some creatures, that live underground, have special nutrient sacks to feed their offspring, Wakasen did not develop these on their chests or stomachs. Instead, our offspring are fed a creamy liquid made from the nutritious natural products of the offshore reefs, which we help cultivate when we are older.

Wakasen are equal to Maken in all areas of life on Inai. After all, why should there be any differences if our brains and bodies are the same? We also have freedom to choose who we bond with. We are careful to make sure we are well matched and can respect each other, so before we join together with a partner, in the Taku-Skani Bond, we have to know them well. Some Maken and Wakasen choose not to bond, especially if they want to dedicate their whole lives to science. As I have said, as our culture is based around space, scientists who study it are the most respected members of our society. For them, nothing is more important than advancing our knowledge.

When I am eighteen orbits, I can go to our local Festival of the Taku-Skani Bond, where we can find a partner. The festival lasts for several days and there is much dancing and celebration of our lives on Inai. My sister went several orbits ago and has now bonded and produced an offspring. She said that it was easy to find the right Maken as there were special places to meet others with the same interests. She prefers to explore space through telescopes, so she met her partner at a telescope camp. I prefer to do it through stories, so I will go to a place where I can meet someone who likes to write about what life could be like on other planets. I can't wait to share ideas with someone about living on worlds completely different from ours. That would be such a strong basis for bonding.

You can go to the festival until you're thirty, but if you haven't found a partner by then you are discouraged from doing so, as it wouldn't be fair on your offspring, as our life expectancy is only about sixty orbits because of the enhanced radiation from our twin suns, which eventually damages how our cells can copy themselves. Some do live until they are nearer sixty-five, but this is very rare, unless they are important scientists and are advancing our knowledge, in which case they are sheltered and cared for underground in special buildings.

I can't imagine living any longer than this in any case. What would be the point, if you already understand our reality as best as you can, and have produced offspring to ensure a viable population of Inaians? You would just be consuming resources unnecessarily, so having a natural limit on our lifetimes is good for our planet too.

So when we are sixty orbits, we say our farewells to our friends, partner and offspring, and make our way to the nearest coast when the tides are right. Along the shores there are special places where we can find a Wat-ot, a very small boat made of large-leafed sea flowers wrapped around thin branches, a traditional design that goes back many, many generations. We attach a picture or drawing of our offspring to our left arm, put some rocks in the Wat-ot, get in and then tie our legs securely to it. In the centre is a hole plugged with a type of sponge that grows on the seafloor and is collected by traditional divers. It holds the waters back until it becomes saturated, and then slowly lets them through, allowing us time to propel ourselves out to sea and drift with the tide.

As the water level rises inside, the Wat-ot gradually sinks beneath the surface and we descend to our last resting place, the seabed, where our bodies provide nutrients for the fish and the undersea plants, which are then harvested and eaten by other Inaians. These are our most important sources of food, along with the nutritious slime that coats the reefs, and which we cultivate to give to our offspring during their first orbit.

We often do this final journey in spindark, so we can look at the Mahpiyai, our beautiful star ocean, one last time before we slip beneath the waves. We call this The Return. As the boat sinks down, carrying us with it, we stare at the picture of our offspring and wish them a happy Path Story. Then we calmly breathe in the seawater and our life comes to a peaceful end. Our bones will fuse with the coastal reefs and we will have returned to nature, to the land under the seas where our ancient prior species came from.

Because our orbit divides up into the time periods for Taku-Skani exactly, we started our scientific journey thinking everything in the universe was also orderly, and that we would be able to find out all the other rules and laws. We called this our Second Age, as our First Age was made up of all our attempts to explain the world around us in old stories, like our stars being our parents. When we have made a mistake and deviated from the path of knowledge and understanding, we sometimes say we have returned to the First Age!

But after we had made the early telescopes, we were shocked to learn of non-double star systems, as we believed ours was the perfect model and so would be everywhere. We also came to think that we lived in the only star ocean, filled up with a fixed number of stars. So our Second Age was full of discovering new things, changing how we thought, and then moving on, sure that the right answers could always be found. But science also journeys on, and seems to be getting ahead of us, and we are now entering our Third Age.

The Third Age is both confusing and exciting at the same time! We no longer know how many star oceans there are, or where the edge of space itself is, or what came before the Great Wakinai, which is why this age is really a challenge to everything that has gone before. We say that in the First Age we believed we knew the answers, in the Second Age we believed we would find the answers, but in the Third we realised that some questions may never have answers.

We don't know what things are ultimately made of, or how the primary force of attraction really works. There is also a big dispute, for the first time in our civilisation, about our development as a species. Some scientists are suggesting we try to alter our inheritance trees to be better adapted to the extra spinlight from our two suns. If this worked then we would have a much better chance of living beyond sixty orbits.

I really don't agree with this interference with nature. We developed to live on this planet, which we love and care for, and there is a natural time for us to leave it and return to the seas to feed the other creatures with our bodies. We are part of the cycle of nature and should not interfere with or try to change it. We gain life from that which went before us, live to learn about space and reproduce, and then give back our particles to the planet to be recycled and reused. Our particles are only borrowed from the planet's store, and must be returned after use.

This is why we are not afraid of death when we make our last voyage out to sea in The Return. We write poems and songs, about what will be our last thoughts as we slip under the waves, and share them with our families. This process has kept our population stable so we don't use up Inai's resources. If we interfere with it, by extending our lives, then we might not want to go through The Return anymore, and a fear of death might come back into our culture, like in the First Age, which would be against everything science has taught us.

One question we do hope to solve, in our Third Age, is how our moon was formed. This has been a question for scientists for many generations. We are living in a very fortunate time as, within the next ten to twenty orbits, we will attempt to land our first exploration capsule on it! Both Maken and Wakasen space travellers will be going, and we are all very excited. When they return, they will bring back samples of the surface rocks, and we will finally know if Petai formed at the same time as Inai from the same materials, or if it came from outside the system, and was captured by attraction. This will, at last, be a big step forward in our Third Age. We will be confident in our discoveries again!

At the moment we only launch small creatures up there, so we can find out how we can be more protected from the rays from our suns. But one day, I am certain Inaians will land on Petai! When I am eighteen I am going to apply to become a space traveller. I can't imagine a better or more exciting future. It will be worth all the long orbits of study and training. Since I was twelve, I have been exercising to be stronger, practising holding my breath for long periods in case of an emergency, and dreaming of walking on another planet or moon! My sister says I should be more realistic, and train to be a doctor, but I feel my future lies in exploring the beautiful solar garden that Makai and Wakasai created for us, and Petai is the first stop on the adventure of our lifetimes. I feel that is where my Path Story leads. And with that, I must end.

I hope you receive my message somehow, and can understand it. Wherever you are, greetings from me, and all of us on Inai. May you live happily until your sixty orbits, and enjoy learning about your area of space as much as I have enjoyed learning about mine. And at the end of your life, remember the farewell our offspring say to us: 'May your body provide the sweetest food for the finest fish!'

***

There was a hushed, tense silence, now heavy with the dead weight of a future that was not to be.

"Try it again," Kan-Ra said.

Rad-Kam tried the switch once more, willing it to work. Just one tiny electrical current to be released around the system, to close the loop and fire the motors that would redeem everything, even as they teetered on the edge of catastrophe. But nothing. Kan-Ra took a deep breath, slowly through her nostrils this time in case that changed anything.

"And again."

Still nothing. After all the triumph, the presumed victory of the equation over the particle, the ever onward, ever upward march of discovery to the drumbeat of scientific progress ... just the dull click of a useless, short-circuited switch. But not just any switch. This was the Kin-Rak switch, named after the mythical rescuer of young offspring lost in the Okagai Lands. It was the emergency option, the failsafe that would ensure that no two space explorers would sit trapped on the surface of Petai. And yet here they were.

The main escape jets had failed to fire through the primary ignition sequence. The engineers back on Inai had designed an entirely separate circuit, completely independent of the first, so the failure of the primary could be compensated for by the secondary. Yet apparently it couldn't. So here they were. Still.

Kan-Ra, a Wakasen from the north. Rad-Kam, a Maken from the south. Fair. Balanced. Unifying. But unifying unfortunately in failure, in a predictable, but previously thought unlikely, fate. They knew which questions to ask, and what the procedures were. And of course, the Kin-Rak switch was the right response to a primary systems failure; there had not been another option. Both travellers were experts in the fields of piloting, navigation, electrical systems, attraction theory... the list of their competences was as long as the summary of the situation was short: hopeless.

"We go forward on the basis that we've missed something," Kan-Ra said. Rad-Kam nodded. There was nothing else to do except play out their roles. Defiance, not submission. The one percent chance always better than none at all.

So back to the checklists, the manuals, the warning lights, the fault codes. The discussions with the voyage leaders on Inai. Teams in mock-up craft back there, carrying out endless simulations. What if this? What if that? Yet nothing. Still they sat. No one wanting – daring – to use the word marooned. But marooned on Petai they surely were.

On Inai, it was as if the temperatures had plummeted everywhere, and the frosts of the extreme north and south were covering the planet with an icy regret. It had been a huge gamble on the part of all Inaians, a gamble of the lives of the two travellers, for the reward of being part of the greatest scientific adventure in the planet's history. And they had all lost. But not as much as the travellers themselves had. The Third Age of Science was indeed not going to be easy, and would have this failure as its first historic defeat. There'd be the descent craft which would become a tomb, and the auto-orbiter, which would revolve endlessly around Petai waiting for the return of the descender. Perhaps there would, in time, be a star named after them. But it would commemorate their sacrifice, not their success.

They had roughly one moonday of air left, one more procession through spinlight and into spindark. And their final decisions to make. Defiance, and sadness. They were lost. Had lost. There was power enough for communication with Inai until just before the end. But before the end could start, they had to say what needed to be said to their families, and these were the worst moments of their lives. Rad-Kam talked to his offspring, his younger brother and his parents, nearing sixty orbits themselves so not too far away from their own Return, but facing the parental nightmare of their own offspring passing before them. Then Kan-Ra talked to her remaining Wakasen parent, her bonded Maken, and her own offspring, who bravely tried to wish her a traditional farewell, but stumbled and broke down before they could get to the end.

Then they were on their own again as a team, for the final time. Trained in the most exacting of survival techniques, and in the mind interactions of fighting the odds even down to the last gasp of the one percent chance, they knew their science had failed them. There were tears in their eyes from the inevitable loss of their families, but also from this failure of everything they had worked for and believed in. Their Path Story had become a dead end.

They both began to plan their final moments. Rad-Kam wanted to climb back down on to the surface and lie on his back, looking up towards the Mahpiyai which they knew surrounded them. Then he would open his helmet to the heavens, and become just another part of Petai's surface, like meteorite debris. It would be as close as he could get to the ritual of The Return on Inai. Kan-Ra had her own plans.

When it was time for them to pass on, Kan-Ra couldn't bear to look Rad-Kam in the eyes. Brave and loyal to the last, he had insisted on going first. He turned around and patted her softly on the shoulder, and she glimpsed the picture of his offspring proudly attached to his left arm. Then, after checking his helmet seal as conscientiously as always, he made his way through the airlock and stepped out of the hatch, so he could walk towards the past that he would soon belong in. Kan-Ra tried not to let her thoughts dwell on the last steps he imprinted on the surface, as he moved past their now abandoned experiments, so optimistically set up just a few short spindays ago on the lifeless, sun-scorched moon. She took calm, controlled breaths, just like her training had taught her, to better cope in challenging situations.

While Rad-Kam lived, she felt there was some inexplicable chance left. But after he'd gone, she would have to confront the inevitability of her being next. It would be soon now. She stared out through the porthole to the side, but saw only the unrelenting blackness of space above Petai's bitter surface. Then her earpiece crackled. It sounded like static, but she knew in her heart it was the sound of the air escaping from Rad-Kam's suit as he'd opened his helmet, and breathed in the stars. So he had gone. Returned. But no point grieving now.

From the compartment where the emergency procedures manual had been stored, she reached for a fading folder she'd brought with her. She pulled out the pages inside it. Setting her voice recorder to readiness she prepared herself, and then began. Reading deliberately and carefully, Kan-Ra went through the words she'd written at school all those years ago. Every last one of them. It was her tribute to her young self, to the person who had powered her way through life with ambition, honesty, and love for her family.

"Hi out there! I am Kan-Ra, and as part ..."

When she had finished the recording, she compacted it, prepared the emergency transmitter to broadcast at full power into the unfathomable depths of deep space, at the setting Rad-Kam had recommended, 1420 xanbits, and sent it on its journey. She had no idea who might receive it, or where, or even when, but she had fulfilled her promise to the Wakasen she had so proudly been, all those orbits ago.

Her turn now. She had gone through what she would do countless times already, turning the tragedy into an operational checklist as best as she could, to keep at bay the despair that would otherwise overwhelm her. Hatch secure. Pictures of her offspring in her left hand, clutched tightly with the unbreakable grip of a Wakasen's proud love. She stared into their eyes, and wished them well for their lives still to come. She remembered the smell of their hair, the sound of their first cries, their first nights when she had stayed awake until spinlight just to listen to their every breath.

Kan-Ra inhaled deeply and slowly. Time to start the last sequence of actions, a commander to the last. She read over them a last time. Turn off cabin lights. Press the Kin-Rak switch as her final act of defiance, her last call for rescue to the saviour of missing offspring. Then hold down the lever to override safety protocol, and depressurise the cabin. And that would be it. There would be no suffering or writhing in her seat. One last pull on the belts that would hold her in place, just like the leg straps on the Wat-ot. She swallowed, but it took longer than normal as her throat was so dry. This was not The Return she had imagined, but it was the only one she could face.

She looked at the picture, and remembered her recent thirty orbit celebrations, with all her family there, and all the hugging and singing and happiness, and rocket-themed cakes and decorations. With her offspring's broken farewells in her ears, about her body feeding the finest microbes on Petai, and their tears in her eyes, she dimmed the cabin lights. Then she reached over to the Kin-Rak switch. Calmly exhaling through her nose to control her emotions, she flicked it for the last time. The engines fired.

***

You sit in your favorite chair for a moment, and look across at the bookshelf in the living room, where your signed copy of Buzz Aldrin's 'Return To Earth' prominently sits in the corner. You recall the shock of the Russian Sputnik satellite in '57, and Gagarin's success in '61, but are proud of how America caught up, and landed those twelve heroes on the Moon. You have been interested in space for as long as you can remember.

You always knew you weren't astronaut material yourself, but high school teaching was a way you could make a living out of talking about science, and the Moon, all day long. You reminisce for a moment about how you met Jenny at a teachers' Christmas party, at that hotel with cocktails at the bar next to the guy at the piano. She'll have been at work for over an hour by now this morning. No long school holidays for her, not since she changed professions!

Your eyes drift to the coffee table in the middle of the room, and the mostly unread copy of June's Astronomy magazine that still lies on it. It has that beautiful sunset on the cover. You wonder if you'll ever finish the sundial project over in the workshop, that sits on your bench in the corner. You've tried to take account of the sun's strange figure-of-eight analemma movement, due to the earth's tilt and its eccentric orbit. And what about latitude? How does that factor in? You sigh, as you already have a big project for the summer. No time for all the extra research and prototypes. Perhaps next summer. You can't even finish your magazine, and haven't dared buy the more recent copies! You smile a little.

You look at your watch, which tells you it's 10:23 am on Tuesday the 16th, and you know that it's time to visit your very own field of dreams. As a summer holiday project, you and the other science teachers have rigged up some old antennae in your school's playing field, next to the lab you share. You hope the array will be able to detect incoming radio waves from a long way away. They are connected to a home-built circuit board on a desk inside the lab, which links to a dot matrix printer. You are really pleased a local company – very kindly – loaned you it for August. It is a few years old now, but it still does the job.

You smile as you remember Jeff telling you, at the end of term party for teachers, all about how he made the board with components from an electronics store in town, and a soldering iron. Then you got your five minutes in explaining how 1420 megahertz was the frequency you were going to look for, because that's what hydrogen gives off, and any aliens sending signals would have worked out that hydrogen was created in the Big Bang, and so was all over the place, so aliens, wherever they were, would know that too, and send messages on that frequency. You joked about how likely that was, and had another beer. End of term, free at last! A surprisingly good staff party, for a change.

You get in your blue '71 Chevy Vega and start it up. You think it's a shame it got all that bad press, and had all those recalls, as you like driving it. There's a bit of a click on the steering as you turn out of your drive, but you'll get it sorted at last when you see the guy at the garage next week. Jeff said it could be the tie-rod ends or something. You're happy leaving it to the professionals. Another week won't make any difference.

The journey to school is uneventful, and after parking you say hello to the receptionist on the front desk, joke about the peace and quiet, and make your way through the pleasantly calm and empty corridors to the lab. You smile when you think of the old line that teaching is the perfect career during the holidays. The printer is spooling out sheets of data methodically into the capture bins, which haven't been emptied since yesterday afternoon, when Jeff was on duty, so you take a huge armful of feeder paper, and roll it out carefully across the front row of desks.

After making yourself a coffee, you put on your reading glasses and get to work. You are looking for anomalies and peaks in the data. You don't expect to find anything, like when you were on watch last Tuesday, but you reassure yourself you are taking part in a real scientific experiment. It's how you should be spending your life.

You, and your colleagues, were disappointed not to be accepted as volunteers for the Big Ear listening programme at the Perkins Observatory site, just off the Columbus Pike near Stratford. The rejection had provided plenty of motivation to see if you could find something they missed! The teacher who finds a message by an alien from far, far away will win a case of beer, so it's a fun incentive. You don't actually like beer that much now you're getting middle-aged, and Jenny has dropped several hints on you slimming down a little this summer, but you played along with the guys as you didn't want to spoil things.

The data on the table is the same as usual. Just read-out after read-out telling a story of a deaf or dead universe. Either that or the alien life forms out there haven't invented tools yet, let alone discovered how to use electronics and radio waves. They certainly wouldn't win against Darth Vader and his Dark Side! You remember the Death Star blowing up in Star Wars, and smile. You have seen the film three times already since it came out a couple of months ago, but will go again in September to cheer yourself up after school re-starts. It is your favorite film of all time.

As an in-joke, you and the other science teachers call yourselves the Jedis from the Dork Side, and you can't help smiling every time you think of it. You shut your eyes and imagine yourself as Luke Skywalker's most trusted wingman. You exchange a thumbs-up from the cockpits of your X-Wing Fighters. But then your mayfly concentration – Jenny says mayflies can concentrate for longer! – flits to the difficulties of interstellar travel, and you remember that *We'll Never Conquer Space* article by that Clark guy, and his view that the vast distances between the stars were unconquerable. That was a downer. Another sigh, and back to work!

Nothing for five to six pm yesterday. Just mindless data. Nothing for six to seven either. Or eight to nine. You go and make another coffee. Nine to 10 is also like looking in a bin full of dud lottery tickets. But when you look at 10 to 11, you almost spit out your coffee all over it.

"What the hell is that?" you think, as you stare at 10:16, open-mouthed. It's unlike anything you've ever seen. There's some kind of jump in the data at about – Oh my God! –1420 megahertz! It starts, increases for about a half-minute and then steadily decreases back downwards into the sea of noise and darkness.

Could it be a signal? You take a breath and sit down. You close your eyes. Just a bunch of high school teachers, eh? Not anymore, if this is right. If that's really what it is. A Nobel prize for you all? Interviews on television? Local press and radio surely at your door tomorrow. But there's nowhere for all the trucks to park. You'd have to do all the interviews at school - probably here in this very lab!

You realize your hands are clenched together with excitement, like a child's fists, and your pulse is a lot higher than usual. No wonder! This would change everything. You can't help yourself thinking what you'd wear for the cover of Time magazine. Your old blue suit one last time, or treat yourself to a new one? And shouldn't the others be with you on it?

They were all part of the project. But do they do group photos? Perhaps just you and Jeff would be better. He did most of the technical stuff, after all. Then again, you found it first. But Jeff's just had a difficult divorce. Imagine missing out on this one. That wouldn't be fair, not at all. You decide to share the moment. But just with Jeff for now.

Then you pause. What if it's not what you think? What if it's just a blip, or a secret air force prototype that runs on hydrogen, or a comet lassoed by the sun and making an unwanted visit like an overly friendly neighbour? You shake your head slowly, as if all the negative thoughts will spill out from side to side.

You work out that if it's a signal, it must have been sent thousands of years ago, and wonder if anyone is still alive on the planet it came from. If only you could reply to them, and explain how their message will turn the world upside down, by confirming the existence of intelligent life in other parts of the galaxy! You pause for a second, knowing that you can't really reply, and the senders of the message will have disappeared – long ago – into their planet's past. The species they came from might even have become extinct, you think, exhaling audibly to yourself in regret.

There's only one thing for it. You are going to take the data sheets over to Jeff right now. He'll be in, as usual, working on something at home in the upstairs bedroom that he's converted to a workshop, and which has old circuit boards hanging from hooks in his shelves, and pull-out wooden drawers full of electronic components. That's where he spends most of his free time since Shelley left and took the kids. His life is about to turn round again! How Shelley will wish she'd stayed. You didn't see her often, but you never really liked her. Neither did Jenny.

You gather up the data pages from 10 to 11 pm last night, put them carefully in a box, and close the lid. There are no copies, so you need to be careful. Right now, this is the most important cardboard box in the country! Then you think of the Big Ear guys. They have a proper set of antennae. You've been to see it. Their gear is huge. They will have caught it all in even more detail! They will be able to confirm everything. One bit of evidence on its own might be questioned, but two sites, independently hearing something, would surely verify it.

A shiver runs down your back. Even if they have found it by now, and are already talking to the newspapers, and television, and President Carter direct from the Oval Office about what they've found, you can back up their results. You might still get a call from Vice President Mondale!

Anyway, first to declare wins. Picking up the box with its paper treasure inside, you make your way towards reception and sign out. It's already 12:35 and Jeff's place is half an hour away. You should just get there for lunch. Jeff does good ham and eggs and that would do just fine. He won't mind making some as he's always pleased to see you, especially nowadays. Lunch, Nobel Prize nomination and then back in time to enjoy that very special meal you're having later. This is going to be a great red-letter day!

The Vega starts first time, and again you think it's not as bad as people say. On the way, you drive past the old Chevy dealer, who had to close his doors after he went bankrupt. Lots of angry customers said he didn't do all the Vega recalls right, and sued him. Much better dealer too on the other side of town, who's giving the car a good going-over a week tomorrow. A truck tractor goes past, and you just know it's an old C-series Ford with the tilt-cab, because the grille looks like a mouth with some teeth missing. You have stopped telling Jenny all about what you see on the road when she's with you, as she says you should be looking where you're going, not trying to work out what everything is!

You stop off at the liquor store for a nice bottle of wine. It is your tenth wedding anniversary, and you want something special for the meal Jenny is cooking you. August 16th 1967 seems quite some time ago now, but you remember the rhyme she told you, about Wednesday being the best day to get married, along with the church, and the vows, and the celebrations – and the honeymoon! – as you peruse the aisle of French wine. The last two years haven't been that good for them, you vaguely remember an article saying, so you head over to the domestic section, and pick up a '76 Californian Cabernet Sauvignon from the 'recommended' shelf. You appreciate giving your mind a break from space, to help you process things a bit in the background, but you know that it won't last long, and you don't want it to. Anyways, back in the car.

You see the red stop light ahead, and brake gently, priding yourself in how smoothly you can pull up. As you sit there, you look up out of the windscreen, and imagine a much darker sky up above. Your mind wanders, and you wonder about the distance between the Earth and the source of the signal you've recorded. You tap on the wheel as your heart sinks slowly, the light years of travel probably reducing the message in the signal to just static, no more meaningful than the background radiation that is everywhere from the Big Bang, a discovery that also rocked your world just over a decade ago. You wish you'd been in on that one! But what if your data is confirmation of something much, much bigger out there than background noise? Your recording could confirm extra-terrestrial life itself! This is the big one!

Then your mind flips back again to the degradation of the message through time and distance, and you sigh, hoping that the Big Ear people have a way out of that. Perhaps the new desktop computers you saw in April, when you visited the West Coast Computer Fair in San Francisco, could be linked together in some way? Could they work on the message and try out lots of ways of decoding it, in case something was there? What were they called? Shacks or something? Pets? Apples? Some strange names for sure.

You think Jeff would know all about them. Shame he couldn't go there, what with his break-up and everything. But you'd taken Jenny instead, so the trip had worked out fine in the end, at least for you two. Your mind goes back and forward. Perhaps the President will ask the IBM people what they can do with the message? Then the light changes.

As you pull away, you check on the back seat in the mirror. The box is still where it should be, with the crown jewels safely inside. The radio is on, and *Horse With No Name* is playing, which you sing along to. It's one of your favorites, and you always find it calming, especially after a tough lesson. You rode a white horse once. Had a mind of its own. Duke? Prince? You can't remember now.

Steering round a bend, you notice the wide, oncoming semi-truck is a little over the line. It looks like a Kenworth, as it has that upright grille you always think looks like a fireplace, and the matching diagonal blue stripes that make it seem as if it's frowning. Its lights are flashing furiously, so you move the wheel a little to avoid it, but the Vega doesn't change its line as quickly as you expect, and you regret the seconds you spent identifying it instead of reacting, when you had more time. You panic now, and try to heave the wheel over, but it is too late.

The brutal slab-sided front of it looms up on you too quickly and it smashes through the edge of the bumper and the hood flies up and you are pitched violently into the steering wheel and blood gushes from your face as the Vega goes airborne and skews sideways into a roll and mortars of shattering glass and screeching steel explode all around you as the road is scraping the roof again and everything is whirling around and you lose track of up and down and you want to scream but can't and the fumes spite your nostrils and you are drowning in waves of blood and pain and there is stillness and silence and the jacket that Jenny bought you is on fire, and then you feel nothing at all.

The Three Jump Surprise

So at the moment I'm just sat here, looking at them. And they're looking at me. They have a trader vessel that's seen better days and I have a modded freighter. I know they're going to die. They know they're going to die. The difference is, I'm still an optimist, because I knew it would end like this and they didn't.

I'm a good mechanic you see. I mean, really good, if I say so myself. I spent a lot of years in the military repairing ships a lot faster and more powerful than theirs. Theirs is just the workhorse stuff. A vessel built for trading in the Solsys. They were good in their day, when they still had squeaky clean engines and drives, but most are a little tired now and not as regularly maintained by their owners.

When I get ships like this in, they always need a bit of work to get them certified as spaceworthy. Lots of them about, but not really meant to travel much beyond our sun's back yard. They're capable of small jumps to higher speeds, but not too many in a row or the engines overheat and shutdown. And if some sneaky mechanic has modified the software sufficiently, everything else closes down too. Including life support. You could call it my insurance policy. When I got good payers, I warned them about it. When I got bad, I didn't.

I always thought that one day it would come in handy. Because bad payers tend to be bad people. And you never know what they're going to do next, because they don't play by the rules. So the good guys have to take precautions. Which I did. And which is why I'm looking at the bad guys right now, through the observation windows on my flight deck.

I'm counting down the time until their life support fails. Not long now. No hurry. Someone once said revenge is a dish best served cold. Minus 270 degrees centigrade in my case, to be exact. The temperature right outside their ship. And eventually, inside it too.

I'm eating a special meal of finest ice lobster, from the subterranean ocean on Europa, with a sauce of rice wine vinegar and ginger butter. And drinking a small glass of a 2056 Chardonnay, which was from a hell of a vintage year. It might all be in packets with tubes, but it's the thought that counts. And I think of them freezing to death nice and slowly quite often. Especially as I can see it happening right in front of my eyes.

I enjoyed my career, right up until I left the service when my stint was up. It had given me a good break from a bad marriage. So when one went, so did the other. Two kinds of freedom rolled into one beautiful divorce. But I don't think about the past much. I prefer problem solving to problem dwelling. I've seen people lose themselves in what should have been. You have to move on from a past you can't change. And I got my fresh start out here, so I guess it all kind of worked out. At least for me.

Things didn't work out so well for Jason though. We had really got on in recent years and I'd watched him grow into a fine mechanic too. But once you make the mistake of getting in with the wrong company, well, bad to worse is assured. The worse becomes the worst. The worst becomes the end of the line. And I'm looking across at those responsible right now. How I got here is a long story. But that's no problem. Unlike the men opposite me, I've got all the time in the world. I can record my memoirs while they're thinking of their epitaphs.

Out here we love our space history. You get a liking for finding out more about the places on your doorstep. Especially about rocks like Ceres, where the main base for the region was set up. First named a planet in 1801. You got to love those old astronomers. What they did with simple telescopes and a few calculations was amazing. They worked out there had to be a planet there, and there was! By 1807, all four main belt planets had been discovered. Nowadays they say it was just a lucky coincidence, but at the time those guys must have felt they were cracking open the universe, one rock at a time. The planets did get downgraded to just objects later on, but that's just semantics out here. The bigger ones sure look like planets when you're flying past them.

The platinum and gold rushes to the asteroids in the 2050s meant there was so much precious metal by the bucketful that the price collapsed back on Earth. All that gold mined on Psyche accounted for most of the collapse by itself. And like with the old Californian gold rushes, bankrupt miners left lots of their equipment behind. Which is where my business in the Asteroid Belt got started. Spaceship salvage and repair. I got together one of the biggest scrapyards on this side of the Belt. The cheapest spare parts for ships, and so much mining gear we almost ran out of bigger rocks to tie it all down on.

Although the first wave of prospecting collapsed, the next wave based around iridium and palladium mining soon got going, and brought in handsome returns. And this generation of miners had plenty of cash to replace things that broke. What they didn't have was plenty of time. A long voyage to Earth and back for spares took a huge bite out of their profits. But with my scrapyard, even if we couldn't pinpoint a problem, we could just swap out things like drive, engine or habitat modules until we found something that worked.

I based the business on an asteroid called 4563G. I liked life there. It was a very useful piece of rock. Lots of asteroids around it within spitting distance. Sure, as an M-type it had some metals and minerals in it. But, unusually, it also had some ice, probably after colliding with a comet or two a couple of billion years ago. Which meant I could get fresh water and oxygen. That saved me half my profits every year alone. And that extra cash gave me enough to pay a good number of assistant mechanics.

So it was just the sweet spot for size. Not too small to have no gravity at all. Not too big to have had volcanoes and magma flows burning off all that ice from those comet collisions in the long, long ago. And nicely balanced between the orbits of Mars and Jupiter, so not too many orbital perturbations to worry about. I was happy to stay right where I was, thank you very much.

After eight years, I'd paid off the investors and the turnover was rolling in, and filling up my account nicely. Of course, some clients preferred to barter. Palladium nuggets were the most used for under the counter deals, but supply swaps were also handy. And both could be off the books.

Applying my military mechanic's training out here was fairly straightforward, as once you've been through the most common problems with ships a few times you know the ropes.

You get your tools together and get familiar with all your diagnostic shortcuts. And there's always people you can ask. We space monkeys are good at sharing like that. And my own guys worked really well as a team.

You know, the first thing that usually goes on those Alcubierre spacetime distortion drives is the frequency oscillators. They're a fairly simple fix as you usually just swap them out for reconditioned ones. I've seen some amazing mileages on the rest of the drive gear.

Then there are the entangled photon projectors, which are essential to the collision avoidance system. These run really hot, and eventually the core quantum matrices build up floaters in their prediction zones. These blur random areas of the course ahead and create a huge risk, as you can't guarantee you're not going to run into an orphan planet or rogue asteroid that comes at you out of a grey zone. And at the speeds you'll be doing, that's going to hurt.

The dark energy harvesters go next. They have filters that eventually get blocked with the wrong kind of negative particles. Again, they're mainly just a swap-out, as you need very specialised, and expensive, gear to get them cleaned up. It's these harvesters that caught my eye some years back now. If they got blocked, then both the front and rear drives shut down, as they couldn't sustain the huge power inputs needed to make the distortion fields work. There was a back-up system, but it was only for local travel in emergencies, like crawling back to Earth from the Moon for repairs on a get you home basis. But they also had a key role in slowing down the ships, as they could vent spare energy back into space and decelerate the ship like nothing else. It put a lot of strain on them, but you needed something like that to slam on the brakes near your destination.

Unfortunately, all that hardware had another flaw. The engineers at the harvester manufacturing bases discovered, to their cost, that if reckless pilots deliberately accelerated and decelerated four or more times in a row, ignoring the cool-down periods, they could cripple both the harvesters and even the main drives themselves. The factories were then liable for repairs under the long-term warranties they offered. So older, high mileage ships were often bought by unscrupulous pilots who did exactly that, cycling through the motions until they got their drives to shut down, usually not too far from Earth or another service station in the Solsys. Then they would haggle with the makers on either replacing the harvesters or drives for free under the warranties, or getting some kind of scrap value for the ship at a fraction of the cost to the factories of doing the repairs. And yes, the scrap value always worked out to be a lot more than the scammers had bought the old ships for in the first place.

After a few kind-hearted conmen alerted them to the fraud, no doubt after some plea dealing, the factories all agreed a limit of four jumps in a row before the hardware defaulted to get you home only. All buyers of ships, and traders of old ones, were obliged to get confirmation from buyers saying they were aware of the limitation. Even so, only two cycles at a time were officially recommended, before resting the ship for a solar day. If you were a legitimate trader, that was plenty.

So that's where I entered the scene. At my repair shop, when I updated the systems, I ran some extra code to limit sudden acceleration and deceleration cycles to three jumps before get you home kicked in. But I also added a total shutdown, even of life support, on the third. I called it never get you home. And if the scammers had planned their fourth jump to get them where they wanted to be, their third could have been to anywhere. And with my surprise in the pipeline, their anywhere quickly became their icy boneyard.

Now you could say that was mean and would catch the fraudsters unawares. And you'd be right. My regular customers, well, they got a good talking to from me about this guaranteed accident. They liked it, because fraudsters weren't the only problem. Over the last decade or so joyriding gangs had proliferated, and they liked to steal ships and push them to the limits. And if there was one thing the joyriders enjoyed it was the four-cycle challenge, taking things right to the edge of what the ships were programmed to do. Then they'd abandon the ship at a rendezvous location where their best buddies would pick them up, leaving the rightful proprietors with a long, time-consuming stripdown if they ever recovered it. So the owners kept my modification as a kind of revenge immobiliser, despite the losses it involved. Sometimes they could even find and recover the ship, and take it somewhere warm to thaw out, jettisoning the frozen joyriders somewhere along the way. It was Top Secret stuff between us all though, as it involved a potentially lethal deception. My loyal crew were also in on it, of course. And my very generous bonuses made sure they would stay loyal.

If a stolen vessel went unrecovered, the insurance guys would have to pay up for it, but the rest of us benefited from getting rid of a whole bunch of criminals. And eventually the fraudsters and joyriding gang numbers dwindled, as more and more of them froze to death in their icy cemeteries. And fewer payouts meant lower premiums. The morality of it all I put away in a locked box in my conscience, and there's no way I'm opening it until long after I retire, and maybe not even then.

Speaking of morals, Jason. He started with me as an apprentice, who I was taking a gamble on. He learned the trade real quick and soon it was like sending a clone of myself on a job.

The other guys got on okay with him, although some said they thought he was a riskier bet than I was used to dealing with. Honest enough at first, he'd do the job well, and also point out ways we could save man-hours by taking new shortcuts, while still billing the full time. He was savvy like that. Too savvy, as it turned out. The more cautious guys had been spot on.

Jason and me hadn't always got on. Family troubles you see. I'd bailed my younger brother out a few times when he'd got into debt some time ago now, and I never forgot how our father's will gave more money to him. That's not how I remembered him talking about what was going to be in it, but I couldn't prove anything so I had to let it ride. But when I needed an extra pair of hands I recruited him to help out. I took a precaution though. I didn't tell him about the Three Jump Limit, and neither did the other grease monkeys. That could wait until he'd proven himself, and put back into the business more than I'd lost out on in the will. When I said I didn't think about the past, that didn't include families. You can leave ex-partners behind, and I have, without a regret in the world, but families can cling on to you like an anxious limpet on a rock when the tide goes out.

After a few years, Jason became responsible for another side of the operation we got into: certifying spaceworthiness. If a ship didn't have a spaceworthy cert then it couldn't get insurance or rescue cover. He was real good at it, and of course when ships were about to fail their cert they'd have to pay us for the repairs. Not a lot of competition out here, you see. Then he got asked by a trading company if they could send some of their ships to us for certification.

We got up to a couple a month at one point, as they were a big outfit. I noticed we were getting billed for fewer and fewer repairs, but as we made it up in the extra cert fees I didn't mind at first. This was about the time that a few of the guys wanted to return to a more lucrative role at the main Mars base, and I couldn't blame them. Plenty of R'n'R there. Then some more asked if they could have leave to attend a wedding together back on Earth. That was another few weeks out of the calendar, so Jason suggested I declare the rest of the month a holiday, shuffle the work schedules and release the rest of the crew, leaving only him and me to finish off the projects in hand. I agreed, and joked he was moving on from issuing certs to running the business!

However, a few days into the new regime, which had felt strangely quiet in the shared areas for a while, Jason got injured, recalibrating a replacement frequency oscillator for a main front drive with an alignment laser. He got a bad reflection in an eye, and had to rest his sight for a while. That cost him several days' work.

During this layoff he got strangely agitated. I said the customers coming back for their ship wouldn't mind waiting, as we were their regular certifying agents. But he said no, it was essential I put the oscillator back in myself before they got there. I'd done the job many times in the past so it was no problem, but I said as he was the authorised cert man he would still have to wait until his eye cleared, and then go back out and check it over himself.

At this Jason became quite angry. We'd never openly fallen out before, as I'd kept the shady will business to myself. I thought we were more than siblings and business partners. I thought, at last, we'd become friends. But he wanted me to put the part back in and pretend that he had done it and okayed it, so he could give the owners their cert when they called the next day. He said nothing else needed done, as it was the last job on the list.

I was really against this. We'd built ourselves a solid reputation, and he was prepared to risk it all if we were found out by the owners. He said he could guarantee there'd be no problem, and not to worry about it. I was so disappointed that our friendship had taken a turn for the worse that my judgement became a bit clouded. I agreed to at least go out and put the part in, and then we could discuss the rest later. That was, of course, just putting off the reckoning, but I thought it would buy me some time until my head cleared and I could work out what I really felt about things.

Unfortunately, what I felt got rapidly worse as I propelled my way through the ship to the drive service bay. I wasn't a cert expert myself, but I'd worked on most things that needed to be passed at one time or another. And I started to see issues. And more issues. And things I would have recommended were changed for the safety of the crew. Things long out of the maintenance schedules. Too many damn things.

I put the replacement oscillator in, rebooted it back online, and started to make my way back through the ship. I stopped off at the ship's bridge, and looked out through the windows at my repair shop. But it didn't seem mine anymore. Things had changed, and badly. I hadn't been born yesterday, and I didn't wish to die tomorrow. I knew what was going on straightaway. The mechanics' signals networks shared messages about scammers, fraudsters and ... gangsters.

Jason had been got at by these traders. They weren't a bona fide organisation at all. They were crooks, running ships on a shoestring and probably using inexperienced and expendable crews to save money and maximise profits. I just didn't know how in on it all he was. But I knew he was issuing fake certs out of my shop. And that hurt like hell.

So before I left the ship, I plugged in my diagnostic module and selected custom update. This way I could install my special Three Jump Surprise and leave no warnings. I didn't have a specific plan in mind, but I knew from now on, one way or another, Jason's cert ships would get the same treatment as all the others. They were faking certs for the cover, but this was my own insurance policy, and it was for real.

I went back and sat down with him. He still had the bandages on his eyes to hold the medication in place. I confronted him with what I'd found out and he caved. He couldn't dispute the evidence I'd found, as it was me who'd taught him everything he knew about the spaceship repair business. And then the story came out. He said he'd had no choice. The traders had explained to him that if he didn't comply, they'd blow up the shop with both of us in it. So he was protecting me too by going along with it. I had to admit he'd done a good job, for all this time, of not looking too anxious about all the blackmail.

If it hadn't been for the laser accident, I might never have realised we were responsible for putting back into space some of the most dangerous vessels around, if Exhibit A sat in the dock was anything to go by. I just sat there, shaking my head at times at this change of fortune. Reality had never looked so mean.

He asked what I was going to do. I didn't know. He reminded me that both our lives were now on the line, so we could just issue the cert and no-one would be any the wiser. I wondered if we could arrange some kind of accident and close the business down. After all, the other guys were all away, and I had enough palladium nuggets stashed away for a rainy day, though I sure wouldn't be sharing any of them with my brother. But I worried they'd just pull the same stunt with another outfit. Or come after us. So I said, as we had a few days before the trader ship with the extra crew was scheduled to show up, that we needed to think it over and even sleep on it a little, as it was going to be one of the biggest decisions of our lives.

Then Jason dropped a second bombshell. He said one certifier wasn't enough for what they had in mind. The top guys were coming sooner than expected to collect their ship, and they would want to have a little talk with me too. They wanted us to leave the service side to their own mechanics, so both of us could be certifiers, as they had another fleet of ships they wanted passed quickly. They were coming to make me this offer and weren't expecting me to refuse it. They weren't the kind of guys you said no to.

Even worse, they were planning on taking me with them to the cert course HQ back on our good old Planet Earth. No doubt they had an angle on that as well. It was basically a hostile takeover of everything I'd spent years to build. But Jason would stay out here and carry on the cert and repair work until I got back. That way he, and the other guys when they returned, were effectively hostages, in case I decided to have a sudden and unannounced change of career back on Earth, and did a runner.

At this point I have to admit I lost my temper and started throwing things around, although with such little gravity not much damage was done. It was one thing to keep me out of the loop to protect me while he was doing the dirty work, but another thing altogether to know that I was about to be roped into the illegal operation as well. If he'd told me before we could have had more time to plan a response, or to get the hell out of there and take our best tools with us. I can't remember ever being so angry with someone.

Now there's movement in the ship opposite. It looks like they're trying for a break-out, as I can see they're all suited up. I'm going to enjoy the wait while they get to the airlocks, and realise they've been disabled in the shut down too. There is a manual airlock, but that's right at the rear of the ship, and by the time they get to it most of their helmets will be flashing low air warnings. So it'll come down to who has the best cardio-vascular system, and can make it all the way to the back. Then I guess they'll try to power over here on max suit thrusters as fast as they can to force an entry. It's a high-risk strategy, but the only one they have. It's that or freeze to death in their cabins or on the bridge. Of course, they're assuming that my ship can't just power up and quit the scene. In their place, I'd be making that assumption too. And I'm not going anywhere until after the grand finale.

They've probably been trying to send distress messages. Unfortunately, their emergency space comms were also disabled by the three jump update, so their words aren't leaving the ship. Like I said, I can be really mean at times. Especially in this situation. I'm declaring dessert time while I wait for the curtains to come down on all the drama opposite me.

When I'd calmed down a little with Jason we tried to work out what else we could do. I had a grand tourer in for a service and it was damn quick on the test run, and full auto too. The nearest cop shop was on 7643F, but space comms were probably monitored by the traders, and message intercepts and diversions were a known problem when calling on the knights in shining armour. The tourer could get there in next to no time.

So I gave Jason an ultimatum. I'd put him in the sleek ship and he could explain to the cops what was going on. They could send the cavalry to rescue me, zap the bad guys until they sang like canaries, round up all the other gang members, and everyone would live happily ever after. Or I'd abandon him here and do a runner in the tourer myself with the palladium, and he

could do all the explaining to the traders about why their
next certifier wasn't playing ball. He didn't fancy that. So off
he went, with only half his eyesight online and the autopilot
doing the skippering through space. He must have felt like
a pirate riding on the Mary Celeste.

While Jason was off on his rescue and redemption mission, I sorted out a modded freighter with boosted drives
that I kept around the back for salvage trips. It had a good
turn of speed and a few other rabbits up its sleeves, and of
course, no Three Jump Surprise. I put a few cases of my
precious nuggets in the hold for the rainy day that might be
coming soon, and took over my grab bag with some survival
goodies, including some special food and drink items in case
things went sour, and I wanted to enjoy my last hours of
being sunny side up in the Solsys.

You can imagine my joy when the tourer returned, with
no sign of the trader vessel as yet. Jason was accompanied
by a patrolman, Lieutenant Dean, who explained that other
patrol ships had been summoned on secure subspace channels and would soon be waiting in hiding for the trader to
get here. Then the miscreants would be arrested and taken
back to the pen on 7643F for interrogation. It sounded a
good idea to me for quite some time. Until, that is, the trader
vessel sailed up to my rock without a care in the world.

Dean looked a bit shifty when I asked him about the cavalry. He said not to worry, they were coming. When the vessel
moored up, I felt like a low-level hum was reverberating all over
my body, which made my heart speed up and my breathing
more clumsy. I'd dropped my guard because Dean had disembarked with Jason. And putting your guard back up was more
difficult if you were trying to do it without it standing out. I
managed some inquisitive looks at Jason, but he was mostly

non-responsive and generally avoided eye contact. I still didn't get it. But I did as soon as the traders came aboard.

Dean had said he'd arrest them as soon as they floated through the airlock. I pretended to myself to believe him, as it was the last hope I had. It didn't happen like that though. Instead, they just offloaded their helmets at the door, and stashed them on the shelves. Dean said we all needed to have a talk, so we propelled our way to a table in the galley, and attached ourselves round the table with the usual cables. It had been clear it was an order and not a suggestion. My heart sank as I looked over at Jason, and everything became obvious. He still couldn't look at me.

"We really wanted you to join us," the head of the outfit said at last. "And we appreciate your community spirit in inviting over Officer Dean here."

Dean smiled and nodded, as though he was receiving a public service award for his loyalty.

I breathed out slowly.

"Jason's been a real asset to our organisation. We were hoping you would be too."

I breathed in deeply and calmly and held the air in for a long moment, letting all the oxygen seep into my bloodstream. Shaking my head slowly from side to side, to fill the gap in the conversation, I discreetly unlocked myself from the table with one hand, while holding on with the other so I didn't float away from my place.

"I worked long and hard to build this business," I countered. "And I don't really have the time, or the motivation, to discuss things with you any further." I knew that would generate a negative response, which covered me inhaling again very deeply, and this time I didn't let it out.

"We were afraid you'd say that," responded the head guy, "so there are some consequences you really need to take on board."

He didn't get a chance to explain any further. Because I quickly tapped the sensor switch, that was taped on to the right arm of my suit, three times in a row. It sent an emergency signal to the galley's life support module. Which blew the decompression seals around the airlock. Which caused all the air in the galley to explosively blow out into space. Which sucked me towards the airlock with it.

Using the last of the air in my lungs, I grabbed my helmet off the shelf, and rammed it on. The others were getting over the shock of the decompression, and trying to make their way towards me, but without any oxygen left in their surprised lungs it was a struggle for them. Their tensioned cables sure slowed them down, until they managed to unclip from the table. I gave my helmet a final twist to lock it in position, opened the first airlock door, moved through the doorway and hit the swap switch. This shut the inner door and opened the outer, ejecting me out sweetly like a cork from a bottle.

I could see through a window that a couple of guys had made it over to the helmet shelves. Not fast enough to get to me though. I grabbed a tether line, and pushed out towards the scooter on the other side of the airlock. Then I attached myself to that instead and sped over to the getaway freighter, with a short detour to attach some mining explosives to the front Alcubierre drive of the patrol ship.

I can see the door has just blown open at the rear of the trader vessel. It looks like one of the guys has made it. He'll be over soon. And what will I do then? Honestly, I'm not sure. We'll just see how far he gets before his oxygen runs out.

The freighter powered up as reliably as always and I manoeuvred it away from my rock. I waited for the explosives to detonate on the patrol ship, which would put it out of action for a very long time. It made a nice pyrotechnic display, blowing a hole clean through the ship's first drive doughnut. Would have been fun to hear that one. And then the great game began.

First drive use across to the other side of this region of the Belt, then power down. And wait. I had to allow time for any survivors of the decompression party trick to helmet up, and make their way to their pursuit ship. Before long, the trader vessel appeared not far away. I knew that, like most ships these days, it had sensing trackers that could follow the trails from my dark energy harvesters, which left a kind of wake turbulence through space, like a ship's propellers churning up the surface of an ocean. Usually you went round them to avoid energy-depleted zones. But you could also tune in to them to follow on in a convoy, like how the first wagon-train missions travelled decades ago now.

Second drive use, this time nearer to 7643F. But not too near. I wanted to give Dean's buddies at the copshop there a challenge, if they wanted to join in with our three jump circus. But Dean had used their only standby patrol ship, and they'd be quite a while bringing a reserve to full readiness. Probably best part of a day. The pursuing trader vessel emerged right between me and the base. Perhaps Dean wanted to wave to his buddies.

Third drive use. This time to the inner side of the Belt, with a good view of Mars in the distance. Like a faithful old pet coming back after being let off the leash, the trader vessel turned up right on cue. And just a few seconds later, all its circuits went offline. I imagined the scene on the bridge as the warning lights all flashed at once, and then the instruments started to power down. As did everything else. Including life support. It's a hard world in space. Especially when you get on the bad side of the good guys.

I can see Dean floating towards me. His spacesuit has patrol markings on it. He's got a grenade in his right hand. Depending on how much oxygen he's got left, he has two choices. He can try to get round to my main airlock and blow it so he can get inside. Or if he's almost out, he can come right up to the screen and pull it there, hoping to breach it, disable my ship, and take me with him. But that's not a revenge dish I'll be sharing with him. He can keep his hara-kiri for two all to himself.

Now he's past the point of turning across to the side and going for the airlock. He must be really short of air then. And yes, the flashing red lights inside his helmet are going off like a panic attack. He must have thought he'd had it made. A few more years of being on the take, and he could have retired to some sunny shore on Earth and never be seen or heard from again. Instead he is going to die out here. But not with me.

I wait until I can see my flight deck windows reflecting clearly in his visor, then I reach down to the energy harvester controls and locate the dump switch. This is something we normally only flip before a service, and a safe distance away from my rock, because it unleashes a wave of energy into space around the ship. I flick it, and the loyal lieutenant is pulsed a safe distance away from my windscreen. Cartwheeling into oblivion, and knowing the game is lost, and he is about to suffocate in agony, he triggers the grenade next to his helmet. Spinning like a silent firework, he has wiped himself out.

I breathe out, and put the harvesters on recharge and recycle. It doesn't take long to get them up and running again. Twenty per cent is enough to kick start the process and once the Alcubierres are humming they get fully juiced in next to no time.

While I'm waiting I think of Jason. He would have had a good chance of surviving the airlock stunt I pulled back on my rock. The best cardio of the group would have been Dean's, being a patrolman. But Jason also had excellent cardio. He had loved diving when he was a child, as had I. Like I said, Jason hadn't just been my business partner, and one-time friend. He had been my brother. And that betrayal of trust was why, when Dean's goodbye had exploded his helmet into the emptiness all around him, I hadn't rejoiced aloud. Whistled with relief, yes, but not rejoiced.

So I don't know what happened to Jason back at the shop. And I don't want to. I carried that sucker of a sibling for far too long. I gave him a future and he tried to rob me of mine, like he robbed me with the will. So fool me twice, shame on me, I guess. But right now I'd rather be me than him. He can carry on being a low-life liar issuing certs worth as much as his sense of honour. If any of the guys return of course, and he can persuade them to work just for him and take care of the maintenance jobs. I'll send them a nice bonus through when I get my relocation sorted, so they don't have to work with Jason if they don't want to have to go along with his idea of doing business. Or, he can just try and escape by himself before the next troop of crooked traders show up wondering where their bosses have gone. I don't know what he'll choose. And I don't care. Another man to leave in the past, just like the other one.

I look out from the cabin one last time and wave goodbye to the trader ship, which sits sullen and frozen dead ahead. No one else made it out through the airlock at the back. I guess they'll be floating around inside their shiny steel coffin for quite some time. Dead to the world.

Me, I'm shortly going to be bound for Earth and somewhere pleasantly tropical. I've heard good things about the eastern coast of Greenland. Palm trees, coral reefs, the works. An old friend of mine said Ittoqqortoormiit was just perfect. Off the beaten track and underdeveloped, not like Kulusuk and Tasiilaq. More hotels there than termite mounds in Brazil. So Ittoqqortoormiit it is.

I end the recording, suck the last of the Chardonnay from the drinks tube, and untie my hair, letting it fall across my shoulders for the first time in way too long. I wish a fond farewell to the Red Planet in the distance, and off to my new life I go. One last jump to one last home. And who knows? I might even find myself another husband.

Shiny Head

On and on the ball ran, always just too far for the boy to catch. It was a lot of fun chasing it down the gentle slope. In the past, he'd have given it a head start, but today it seemed to have a will of its own, and every odd bounce down the hill put it further from his grasp. It came to a rest just past the old tree at the bottom of the hill, in the far corner of the field. He usually tried to avoid being too near the tree, after what had happened when he was younger, but the ball went there, so he did too.

Breathlessly, he slowed down, knowing the duel was over and the ball had won. He walked towards it, sucking in the air with relief and calming down, as his heart started to beat more gently. Reaching down, he grasped the ball with enclosing hands, brought it back up to his chest, and took a good look at it, as if greeting a long-lost friend. Then he turned around. He stopped dead in his tracks, as if the world had been shattered by the complete shock of seeing what was in front of him.

It made no sense whatsoever. He searched his young mind for memories or images that might help him understand what he was seeing, but there were none, because this event had never occurred before, and so had never been seen by anyone. The boy out playing in the fields next to his home had simply expected, after picking the ball up, to have a peaceful little walk back up the hill, perhaps glancing at the odd rabbit poking its head out of the hedge, to check if it was safe to warm itself in the yellowing sunlight and gentle westerly wind.

He looked around him, as if to appeal to other witnesses, and to say, *Look, there is this thing in front of me and I don't know how it came to be there*, or, *How is such a thing possible?* But there was no one else to see what he could. Even the families of sparrows, that sang in the hedge bordering the bottom of the field, were unusually silent. And so was he. He blinked and looked again. The tree was still there. As was the front half of the body of a man sticking out of the trunk.

He had never seen anything like it in his life, and instinctively knew that he never would again. *There was a man in the tree.* Not next to it, not in front of it, but actually half inside it. He stepped closer, willing each step onwards and desperately trying to be quiet. The upper half of a man's body was sticking out of the tree trunk, face downwards, at about his waist height. The lower half, although the boy could believe his eyes even less, was somehow enclosed within the tree. It was not just squeezed into some kind of bored-out hole, but inside it, in the sense of being part of it. The trunk was closed up around the body like it had grown with it, like it had always been there and was a part of the tree. The head seemed more out of place than anything else, being completely bald, and, in the warm rays of the late afternoon sun, even a little shiny, as though there was more to it than skin and bone.

Almost on tiptoes, he crept round the back of the tree, where two large feet stuck out. He looked at them closely, thinking that if he'd been younger, he'd have had the temptation to tickle them. Then he noticed something really odd. The feet had no toes. Instead, there was just a darker, thick ridge of skin. It looked quite solid, like the edge of a club-like weapon of some kind, as though the feet could be used to kick down doors or break things up. Then he twisted around cautiously and started to creep back around the front. He squatted down slightly to get a better look at the man's face. Its eyes were closed, but it seemed in no pain.

And then he realised more things, quickly, in a jumbled order of thoughts. It had no clothes on either its upper body, or its lower legs and feet. It was bizarrely sticking straight out of the tree, not slumped downwards. He stared again at the thing's chest, but it definitely wasn't moving. Nothing made sense. Although it wasn't breathing, somehow it didn't look like it was dead. He didn't have that awful feeling of being next to a dead person that he'd only ever known once before. This time he was able to stay strangely calm, although even he didn't know how.

He scrunched up his eyes and rubbed them. He felt like he was stuck in a story in one of his favourite manga comics, until the following month when the sequel would come out. Or perhaps he had bashed his head on a rock after falling down the hill as he was running, and he was just hallucinating. His mother would come and take his hand, and he would go back to his bedroom, and he'd have a long sleep and it would all be over.

But he wasn't in a comic, and it wasn't any kind of dream. Not at all. There really was the upper torso of a man sticking out from the front of a tree, and not just any tree; this was the tree with the most importance for his family of any tree in the world, and the man's feet were sticking out the back of it. He wondered if he would ever understand it.

Even his mother would probably have difficulty explaining it. If he told her. But while only he knew, he apparently had one of the world's biggest secrets all to himself. He was still young enough for that to appeal to him, and he shivered at the thought. This was one of the most exciting things that had ever happened to him. He didn't know what it meant, or where it would lead, but this was a very special thing. And right at the end of the summer holiday too. Keeping it a secret from his friends would be easy. Because he hadn't had any for a long, long time.

In the distance, a voice called his name, and he took a last look at his new project and turned away, jogging back up the hill just as he'd done when his dad was there, running uphill with him, and telling him how good it was for your heart and lungs, and how it put some grit in your legs. He still missed him terribly.

Dinner with his mother went well, and he feigned interest in the usual questions about what he'd been up to, and whether he'd seen any animals today. He never mentioned the tree, even though he normally spent a good deal of time climbing it, and looking out from the branches into the woods. Especially that branch. He would lie on it and hug it. Before leaving it, he would say goodbye, make his way down the trunk, and then give several pats to its rough bark before turning away, as if he could share his sorrow with it and this would somehow make it less. It was the closest contact he could ever have, after what had taken place there.

But today something had changed. The tree didn't just belong to him and his mother now. And he appeared to have found another dead person there, who wasn't breathing but didn't seem dead, sticking out from the trunk. Not higher up, gently swaying in the breeze. Then he'd screamed all the way back up the hill. Now he was quiet about it. Then, everything had been taken away from him and he'd lost something forever. This time he would deal with things in his own time. When he'd decided what to do. He realised his mother was no doubt wondering what he was thinking about, and was probably about to ask him, so he yawned noticeably and claimed to be tired out and kissed her goodnight, and went up to bed.

He went to sleep surprisingly quickly given the day's revelation, but it didn't last, as always in his world when something in it loomed larger than normal and was unresolved. By the early hours he was awake again, listening to the first drops of rain on the skylight.

He went to a window, and looked out towards the field with the tree with the man half inside it. Fairly soon it was pouring, and the rain noisily flooded down the windowpane, as if attempting to wash away his secret, until he could see no more. He tapped his phone to get the time, but there was no battery left, as usual. He took no interest in phones, or the internet. Not after all the lies that had spread on it. And what had become of the victim of those lies. His father.

Despite knowing it was wrong to go out in the middle of the night, he couldn't help himself. He was at the beginning of what he felt could be the biggest adventure of his life. It was not time to tell his mother. Not yet. There was a lot more finding out to do first. He wanted to figure things out by himself.

He dressed quickly and took his own time getting downstairs, avoiding every creak in the telltale stairs. The back door out of the kitchen was the quietest, so he went out that way, covering himself with a small tarpaulin from the shed. They'd once used it to cover the kennel in the garden when they'd had a dog, and the roof had leaked in the rain. But the kennel had long since gone, and so had the dog.

Before too long, water was streaming down his face, and by the time he was halfway down the slope he was soaked through, despite the tarpaulin over his head and shoulders. The track was reasonably smooth, and there was just enough light to see by, as the dull glow from the nearby Meadowpitch floodlights bounced lazily off the low rain clouds, and spilled into the field. He could hear the rain spattering onto the leaves of the trees that bordered it, and he carried on down to the corner, careful to tread where there were clumps of grass to still provide some grip, to where the biggest tree was. In summer showers he had sometimes sheltered under its branches during the day, but this was the latest he'd ever been out. He could hardly remember ever being awake at this time of the night, let alone being dressed and outside.

Rounding the base of the tree, he could make out the shape of the human form sticking out of the trunk. The streams of water were channeling down rivulets in the gnarled old bark and pouring off the man's back, from where they teemed onto the sodden ground. For the first time he felt sorry for the thing in the tree. It was still bizarrely horizontal, and nothing seemed to have changed. He felt a pang of sorrow, and after slowly taking off the tarpaulin from around his shoulders, he carefully laid it over the man's back and head. It felt the right thing to do.

He stood quite close to it and wondered if he should really be getting back to bed now, as he wasn't having much of an adventure anymore. It just felt very cold and wet, standing there in the faint glow from the Meadowpitch lights in the distance.

And then the man's right hand shot across and grabbed the boy's leg just above the ankle, with a vice-like grip. The boy let out a noise the like of which he'd never heard before and which surprised him, a sort of gasping half-scream of panic and shock that should have come from a wild animal caught in a trap, but instead projected uncontrollably out of his own throat.

"Let go of me!" he managed to blurt out, but the words seemed joined together and didn't come out right. The grip tightened, and the pain became unbearable.

"Let go," he pleaded again, breaking into panicked breaths he couldn't stop, "I tried to help you!"

The thing reached out with its other hand and grasped the tarpaulin, slowly pulling it off to one side. To his horror, the head, so conspicuously still in the first encounter, was moving haltingly towards him, as if it was rotating on a slipping cog, to what seemed the limit of the movement of its neck. And then it opened its eyes. Another gasp of terror left the boy's body. He looked down and the two sets of eyes met. He had expected to see glowing, devilish eyes that would try to draw him in to some kind of trap, but once he'd refocused, he saw only water streaming over its eyebrows and down over the two dull, shadowed, empty spaces below. Then, a second later, its face seemed to go blank, and the eyes closed and the grip relaxed.

Seizing his chance, the boy pulled his leg away and stepped backwards. Taking a deep breath, he ran hard back up the hill, hoping all the way that it would not be able to free itself, and catch him before he got to the safety of his garden gate.

When he reached it, he tried to gather himself together. He breathed heavily into his sodden jacket, fearing that all the world would be able to hear his erratic gulping of great mouthfuls of saturated air. He hid his soaken shoes in the garage so his mother wouldn't find them, and got ready for bed again. It felt like hours before his heart had calmed down enough for him to fall asleep.

The boy decided to return to the tree at the bottom of the field as soon as his morning's chores were completed. Last night had been an adventure for him, but it had all gone so badly wrong. He had stood too close to the man, who was obviously not dead at all, despite everything.

This time he walked down the hill. As he got closer, he dropped on all fours and crawled just above the ground by the hedge, as quietly as he could, to the puzzlement of the butterflies he disturbed, which were warming themselves up on the September dandelions and daisies. He set up position slightly behind and to one side of the man, so he couldn't be seen.

The shiny head was looking around in the sunlight, as if straining to hear, like an animal rotating its skull to get the best input into its ears, so it could fix the direction of incoming sounds. The boy watched from a distance, breathing softly and waiting for something to happen. He didn't have to wait long, but nothing happened as he could have expected.

Silvery pearls started to appear on the man's feet and trickle off onto the grass below, and small wisps of smoke carouseled up into the air from where they fell. The boy looked around him but there were no clouds, and it was too late for the mist that sometimes floated above the fields first thing.

Then more droplets fell, and soon each foot was pouring out molten metal, which reminded him of the experiments he'd seen of mercury flowing like a magical fluid. Then he realised the man's feet themselves were melting. He had no idea how this was happening. Perhaps the man was heating them up himself? Like minute waterfalls of flowing steel, the outpourings glowed hotter and redder until they looked like two streams of lava. It was as if the tree had burrowed its roots into an underground volcano, and was now undergoing punishment, with an angry chamber of magma unleashed through the feet of the strange being imprisoned in the trunk.

The boy was astonished. He now knew that the thing was not human, lived without breathing, and could melt off its own feet without feeling any pain. But how would his mother ever believe what he was seeing with his own eyes, right in front of him?

The dissolving process continued to devour its way up the man's legs, until a heap of bubbling metal lay on the floor at the base of the tree trunk, as if shiny metallic coral had started to grow there. Soon, both leg stumps had gone, and the streams of pouring metal merged, and the man's hips and lower body also began to melt down, glowing in the centre of the tree like a furnace. The new outpourings ran down the trunk and over the top of the glinting, glowing coral below.

There was a crackling and popping as the wood inside the tree, which had merged with the man in a way the boy couldn't understand, also burned, and a column of smoke began to rise up and around it, and the embers glowed brighter in the gentle breeze, as if promising that the morning would end with the whole tree ablaze.

The smoke pouring out from the trunk was too much for him. He crept backwards and then turned round, running up the slope as fast as he could. Their tree was on fire! He had to tell his mother. He had to warn her. She would know what to do. The secret adventure had gone too far. His chest was burning from the effort of the running, and his leg muscles grew tauter as he raced on until he felt the tendons would snap, but he didn't stop. There was enough grit in him to get right to the top of the hill.

At the bottom of it, the being trapped in the tree was about to escape. His arms reached out towards the ground, and he steadied himself. With a last cloud of smoke from the trunk's hollow, the front of his body, no longer attached to anything else, rolled out of the front of the tree and onto the ground. He was free again, but the freedom had come at huge physical cost.

Lying on his back and looking up at the sky, he pushed and prodded his still smouldering lower torso with his hands, until he seemed satisfied with its newly improvised enclosure. Then he turned over and pulled his way over to the still damp tarpaulin, left close by from the previous night's encounter with the boy. He dragged it back across to the tree, and started to stuff it into the hole in the trunk. Propping himself up with one hand, and pivoting on his newly smelted lower half, he rubbed the covering with his other hand against the burning heartwood, the moisture on it soon putting the struggling flames out, until only acrid grey smoke remained.

Then he took a firm hold of the molten metal reef at the foot of the trunk, and dragged it towards the bushes near the hedge. One hand was digging fingers into the soil and pulling his body along, like rowing his way across a dry seabed, while the other grasped and pulled the dead weight of his melted body parts behind him. With his exposed skin seemingly unaffected by the unwelcoming mass of nettles and thistles, he settled deep inside the undergrowth and closed his eyes.

By the time the boy and his mother – who was desperately clutching a small kitchen fire blanket more in hope than reason – reached the tree, there were only wisps of smoke from the dying embers of the fire within the strange hollow in its trunk, now partly filled with the old tarpaulin. Which was recognised by his mother instantly. But the man had disappeared. And so had the pile of melted metal. The boy couldn't believe his eyes for a second time. He didn't know what to think about anything now. And then his mother's questions came tumbling out.

"What on earth went on here, Sam? Why is the tarpaulin from the shed inside a hole in our tree? Did you do this? You know how important this tree is for us. Did you cause the fire? Why would you do such a thing?" It was his mother's turn to be in shock, and out her questions poured without waiting for his responses, her head shaking from side to side in disbelief.

"But I didn't do anything," the boy said in exasperation, while understanding that no matter what explanation he came up with, he wouldn't be believed, because in truth nothing that he'd seen was believable.

"Were you trying to cremate the tree as well as your dad?"

His mother knew straightaway she'd gone too far, but was too upset to hold back. Within an instant, she saw his pained reaction that she would think such a thing. The boy crumpled up into a heap on the floor, and his tiredness and shock from the previous day overwhelmed him.

With a little more sympathy this time, a lower voice, and her hand on his shoulder, his mother continued, "Did you do this Sam? Did you set fire to our tree?"

She couldn't believe there was such a deep hole in it, with no obvious way to explain it, but she had to ask, had to know more.

"No!" Sam shouted back. "No, I didn't. It wasn't me! It's my tree too and I'd never harm it. I wanted it to live forever."

As he sank back to the ground, he knelt and rested his head forwards on the damp grass. Although he tried to hold back his emotions by gritting his teeth, the sobs just broke out through his nose instead. He felt even more embarrassed at this, as though he had gone from having the best secret in the world, to knowing deeply embarrassing things that he could never say, and which could only lead to further trouble. He didn't know what to do.

If he told her what he'd seen, she'd think he was hallucinating again, like after his dad's death, and there'd have to be more counselling, and more sleeping pills, and more distant relatives he didn't really know giving him hugs, and telling him every-thing would be all right, when he knew it never would. Or he could stay silent and leave it all unexplained, which was like taking the blame for it anyway, and having it come between him and his mother, the only person left in the world that he could trust.

The tree was the last natural link to his father, and he would never have harmed it. Surely his mother should have remembered that? He had explained to her how, when he touched it, he somehow felt a connection to him, as it was the last thing his dad had ever touched before his leap into the past. And now their sacrificial totem pole had a huge hole in the middle of it, and he didn't know whether it would ever recover.

He stood up and looked around him. There was still no sign of the man. He looked at the floor, and regretted that all the molten metal had gone, leaving only a burnt patch of grass which proved and told of nothing. But at least his crying had stopped.

His mother walked around the tree slowly, eventually pulling out the tarpaulin and checking the fire was out. She shook her head slowly.

"I don't know if it'll live," she said reluctantly. "I don't know if trees can survive this sort of damage to the heartwood." The tears welled up in his eyes again. She put a hand on his shoulder again, and then, as if she was taking the biggest gamble of her life, looked him in the eyes.

"Okay," she said, deliberately calmly this time. "You know, don't you? You don't want to tell me, but you do know what happened?"

He nodded.

"But it wasn't your fault?"

Sam nodded again.

"So if it's not your fault, you can tell me." Although he tried to say that he could, but she wouldn't believe him, it just came out as rambling gasps for air between half sobs, as he tried to catch his breath and stay lucid, but it was as if time had broken up and was now fractured, like a dropped mirror that he was using to make sense of his reflection, piece by shattered piece.

But it was reality itself he couldn't make sense of. He knew what he'd seen, but nothing else he knew could help him understand it. He took a deep breath and hugged his mother like he was a toddler who'd lost her on the street, and then found her again, while in the midst of a blind panic. She was there for him. Again.

"You wouldn't believe me," he eventually managed to say, as if he had to stick the words together in his mouth before he uttered them to make sure the sounds came out in one joined up piece. But then he kept repeating them, and like a runaway train they seemed to take him over and he just stood there shaking his head.

"It's okay," she comforted him. "It's okay. Try me. Trust me Sam. Tell me."

He took a big breath and was about to start with the ball running away from him down the hill, but he didn't have to, because at that moment there was a rustle in the bushes behind him, and what remained of the man pulled himself out along the floor, and then looked up at them both.

"Help me, Emma," it said, slowly and deliberately.

His mother screamed so loudly he thought his eardrums would explode.

The journey back up the hill was just as surreal for both of them. Sam had gone back and brought the wheelbarrow down, and they had helped the man pull his cleaved and riven body into it. They'd partially covered him with the tarpaulin, in case anyone else was out walking nearby. Then Emma had lifted the handles and, with Sam helping as best he could, they'd all set off for the house. The man looked ahead, from under the cover, like a broken figurehead from an old sailing ship she'd rescued from an abandoned dockyard. She had given him just one chance to explain who, and what, he was when they got to the house, or she'd call the police. He'd just nodded in agreement. He didn't seem to have a lot left to lose either.

So they were all gambling on the way back up the hill. She had absolutely no idea how he knew her name, and when she'd asked what they should call him, he didn't know. It all felt like one of the greatest mysteries of her life was starting, with everything centred on the surprisingly heavy half-man – or half not-man? – they were both resolutely pushing uphill in the wheelbarrow.

Sam saw no animals this time, and heard no birds. It was like they were all separate from nature for once. He had felt robbed of his secret when the man had emerged from the bushes and greeted his mother. But although there'd been excitement over the untold story fermenting inside him, there'd also been a growing sense of anxiety. Now his mother knew, the panic was slowly flowing out from him, and ebbing away with each footstep planted uphill in the still wet grass, though somehow he felt there was a lot more strangeness to follow.

When they were back at the house, Emma offered the chance for their visitor to recharge in some way, but he just shook his head. He seemed to be a very self-contained kind of half-man, with no visible recharging ports, unless they went in through his ears, which Emma had wondered about briefly. She offered him something to wear, but that was also declined.

She didn't feel threatened anymore, but she wasn't sure why. Perhaps it was just the brute fact that he had only his upper torso, and so was extremely limited in movement. They could walk away from him any time they liked, and that was reassuring. His skin looked human enough, except for the dull and lumpy metallic layer that sealed up his lower frame, and his head and face could easily pass for a human at first glance, despite an artificial-looking sheen from some angles. His eye movements and facial expressions seemed little different from a real person's, although sometimes there seemed a strange kind of syncing delay.

She'd never seen anything like him. Except for once. Emma cleared her throat meaningfully to herself as she realised. Years ago, she had taken a first aid course, and had to breathe air into a dummy torso with a lifeless head. Yes, he was like that. Living in his own peculiar way, without breathing of course, but undeniably similar.

Emma made herself a cup of tea, following the very English protocol for coping with shock or unease, and poured some lemonade for Sam. The man had pulled himself up onto the sofa and lay there, as if trying to work out his explanation for the mystery that had just upended their lives. Then he began, in an articulate voice that seemed bizarrely at odds with the propped-up half-man from which it came.

"Emerging in the tree was not planned. Losing my lower body was not planned." He paused, but it was not to draw breath. "There is still something I have to do. That is why your help is needed."

"And this important thing is...?" Emma asked, making an encouraging gesture with her hands for him to continue.

"Meadowpitch will be attacked soon. This has to be prevented."

Emma's eyes opened wider. Meadowpitch was where her husband had worked. It was a nuclear waste reprocessing centre that had seemed cursed from start to finish. And why everything had gone so wrong in their lives the previous year. And now something else was going to go badly there? She started to listen intently.

"Acts of sabotage will cause a huge fire, and there will be radioactive pollution, which will devastate this country and much of northern Europe."

Sam and his mother exchanged a nervous glance. It was precisely the sort of thing his father had tried to warn people about. It sounded like the end of the world for them. Again.

"So you're saying you know all this because you've got a crystal ball, or you're from the future and you've got a time machine?" Emma asked, not sure if she should sound concerned or sceptical, and trying to use a tone of voice that was somewhere between the two.

Sci-fi wasn't her favourite genre, but it had been her husband's, and she had seen more than her fair share of those types of films. She also knew that the talking torso in front of her wasn't from any present that she was aware of. But Sam had played computer games where travel through time was exactly what took place. And after what he'd seen the man do to his own body to escape from the tree, he guessed the future was involved somehow.

"But how," asked Sam. "How did you even do it? How did you get here? And why did you end up in our tree?"

"Then you tell us about Meadowpitch," Emma added. "I want to know everything about what happens there."

"You are right about the future," the man began. "Scientists try to stop the devastation by preventing the explosion. They use a new generation of quantum-squared mainframes, or QSMs as they are named, to work out how to send a robot back to this place at this time, and arrive in a clear area of the field. They use this field and the tree as a reference point, because it still stands thirty years in the future."

Emma felt a wave of relief break over her chest. So the tree had survived after all. She and Sam looked at each other and she could feel her eyes well up, with the remission from the fear of the tree becoming an open sepulchre.

"Unfortunately, there was an error," he continued. "The target zone was ten metres to the east of the tree, but there were millions of calculations. The error in one of them meant my arrival was too far to the west. Inside the tree. Escaping it cost my legs and lower body. But the sabotage must still be prevented. With your help, it can be."

Emma looked at Sam, as if to say this was already so unbelievable that they might as well hear the rest of it, and it reminded her of reading him bedtime stories when he was younger, with magic and sorcery and dragons. The stories weren't much less believable than what the talking upper torso of a half-man from the future was saying. But another part of her knew she was already convinced, and had been since he had crawled out from behind a bush and used her name.

"Go on," she said, slowly and supportively. "So what exactly happens at Meadowpitch?"

"After a fire, the plutonium fuel dumps at Meadowpitch explode, poisoning northern Europe with radioactive particles. There is chaos, panic, and mass migration southwards, until the southern countries close their borders, and then there is huge conflict and suffering."

"But how?" Emma reacted angrily. "How could they let all that happen? They said it was safe. They hounded my husband out of there and said he was scaremongering. But they lied, didn't they? It wasn't safe at all. It was just as vulnerable as he said it was."

"Your husband was right. Three countries working together hacked all the safety systems. They used bribery, blackmail and death threats to key personnel to get passwords. It took years for them to get everything in place. The hackers chose their target well. They picked the nuclear site with the worst safety record, software vulnerabilities, and managers."

"So when does it all kick off, and how?" Emma was totally absorbed now in the man's story. Sam looked on, trying to make sense of what he too was hearing, even if he didn't understand all of it.

"Very soon. When the weather is right, the sleeper viruses installed in the operating software at Meadowpitch are activated. Sprinkler systems are turned off, and water tanks emptied. Computer cooling systems are disabled, and their CPU's overclocked, so most of them overheat and cause widespread fires.

"The communications systems and utilities of the nearby town have also been hacked, so most police and fire vehicles are stuck in huge traffic jams and are unable to get to the complex. Those that do can't get through the main gates, as they are locked down as if the base is under a terrorist attack, which it is, but from the inside."

Sam was already open-mouthed at how people could deliberately do such stupid, reckless things. Emma gave him a hug, while slowly shaking her head in dismay. She knew this was only the start of the plan. And sure enough, the man continued.

"Then the real damage starts with the draining of the pools that contain tonnes of highly radioactive sludge. The managers had destroyed the records of what was in it, so it is much more dangerous than the workers realise. The sludge pool overheats and explodes, demolishing the walls of the buildings next to it that contain most of the plutonium stocks. When these are compacted together by the walls and roofs collapsing, chain reactions occur and there is an explosion which ejects radioactive particles high into the atmosphere. It is the biggest nuclear disaster in history.

"Worse than Chernobyl?" Emma asked in shock, just to be sure, but already guessing the answer.

"Yes. Twenty-six kilogrammes of radioactive material escaped from Chernobyl. Meadowpitch releases one hundred and fifty tons of plutonium. The attackers choose the date of the attack from the weather predictions, and a strong northwesterly wind disperses radiation from here to Munich. This effectively cuts Europe in two.

"Agriculture and livestock are devastated by the fallout. Soon, a third of northern Europe is hungry or sick from radiation. There is chaos, as millions of people try to evacuate themselves to the south. Britain collapses into anarchy. Its security and military are totally overwhelmed, and the north and most of Scotland become uninhabitable for decades."

Emma instinctively looked towards her kitchen knife drawer, but she knew in the face of a complete breakdown of law and order there was little they could do to protect themselves for any length of time. She had stopped her husband, in his last weeks, from covertly buying a shotgun from the farmer next door when he had the chance, and now she didn't know whether to regret this or not. But all that would no doubt only delay the inevitable. She was beginning to feel overwhelmed by the scale of the coming catastrophe.

"Is that it? Surely it doesn't get any worse."

"The hacking powers had decided to create a disaster in Europe to overwhelm the west, and provide cover for their plans to conquer and annex other countries. So these aggressive states, and others, take advantage of the chaos to invade their target territories."

"And all that from a hacker attack ... on the Meadowpitch complex?"

"Yes."

"My husband was more right than I'd ever realised, until now." Emma sighed. "Do you know about him?"

"Yes, my programming includes the names and addresses of most of the scientists connected to Meadowpitch, and their families, in case their help was needed."

"And you know he tried to warn others about the dangers there?"

"Yes. He was blamed for some missing plutonium."

"He was framed. They wanted to get rid of him because they feared he was becoming a whistleblower, and would alert everyone to the horror show at that place. With the loss of his job, he also lost his purpose in life. He became depressed, and we couldn't get him out of it. He couldn't believe how the other scientists at the site had turned their backs on him. Then there were rumours and lies on the internet, connecting him to terrorist groups, and Sam got bullied at school. And in the end, David could see no way out, and ended his life. On that tree you just emerged out of."

The man nodded.

There was a very heavy pause. Sam felt overwhelmed by everything, especially hearing again about why his father had died, and after giving his mother's arm a comforting little squeeze, he went upstairs to lie down on his bed for a rest. But he left his bedroom door ajar, so he could still hear most of what was being said downstairs.

Emma thought for a while, aware that she was trying to hold back some of the memories from the half-man from the future propping himself up on the sofa opposite. But she couldn't hold back all of them. It had been so long since she had talked to anyone about what happened. And somehow his bizarre appearance helped her unload, as there were no cues for her not to.

"David's death almost broke me. If it wasn't for Sam, I would have joined him on that branch. I thought I knew my husband, until the day I realised I didn't. It was too late then. If I'd really known him, known about the depths of his depression, and that when he talked of 'the end' he meant his own, I might have been able to change things. But I don't know about you either. So who, or what, are you? What can you tell me about yourself?"

"The team that made me decided going back in time would kill a human being," he responded. "They didn't even know if a robot could survive. The man who programmed me gave me his voice. He was called Jeremy, and he said hearing me was like hearing himself. The team named me Jed in his honour. All of that so the destructive explosion could be stopped. But the tree has changed everything. There is only enough power inside me now to complete the last part of the mission. Melting away my lower half used up a huge amount of my stored energy. There is none left in reserve to get from here to the complex. Not like this. That is why your help is needed."

Emma looked up at the ceiling. The thoughts churned through her mind, and then she gave the answer he'd been waiting for.

"Yes, I will help you do what you have to do. But why can't we just warn Meadowpitch?"

"Jeremy programmed me to deny that option. He said there were too many compromised staff. The hackers would launch the attack as soon as they suspected the plan had been uncovered."

Emma had gone as far as she needed to. She cared more now about Sam not getting fatal radiation poisoning, so she wanted to get back to the when.

"And when do you think they want to do it?"

"The forecast says the wind now builds and swings round to the northwest, and is strongest on Sunday night, so that's when the hacking starts."

"But that's tomorrow!"

"Yes, and it's when the hackers know the staff at the centre are lowest in readiness and numbers. That's why the team sent me yesterday, as close to the event as possible to reduce the uncertainty of the arrival coordinates."

"So how do you plan to intervene and save the world – or at least our part of it?"

"There's a river that runs alongside, and then through, the complex. The new approach uses a back road that gets close to it. You need to get me to the drop-off point in your car. From there, it's just downstream all the way. The river will make me colder, and help shield me from thermal cameras. Pulling myself along the river bed will get me to a support column that can be climbed to an overhead gantry, which goes over the top of the main radioactive sludge pool they're going to target. Robots don't need oxygen or have organs affected by radiation, so I can access the pool from there. The hackers will set off the first stage of disruption and chaos to distract the workers. Then they will execute the hack."

"To cause the draining of the pools?"

"Yes. The one full of radioactive sludge next to the plutonium stores is the main target. When they open its sluice gates the cooling water will flood out and the sludge will self-ignite in the air soon after that. The gates must be sealed, to stop them opening."

"How will you do that? And how will you escape?"

"By melting myself into them. They'll be welded together and never be able to open again. There is no need for an escape plan."

"That definitely sounds like suicide."

"Robots cannot commit suicide. We do not have lives to end. All the programming from Jeremy that has come back with me will be lost. But this body is disposable. For the mission to succeed, it has to be. There's no other purpose to my being here."

"So you're going to end your life without a regret in the world?"

"There is no life of my own to end, or to regret."

The door pushed slowly open. Sam, who had obviously been listening, stood there, a tear rolling down his cheek.

"Can we bury the metal from your legs?" he asked. "Next to where we put Dad's ashes?"

Emma smiled. "That's a good idea," she said. "And can we call you Jed?"

As they pulled into the lay-by, Emma knew her life was about to change again, but this time for the better. If he succeeded. She looked across at him, still securely pulled into his seat by the belt.

"I have a favour to ask," she said. "I'm never going to see you again, but there's something you could do that would really help me – apart from sacrificing yourself to avoid a nuclear waste disaster. That's already quite a lot, of course," she went on with an awkward smile.

He looked across at her. She knew that behind his eyes was a special type of computer and not a human brain, but sat there, looking across at him, she thought he was about to do a very human thing: to sacrifice himself for others, a selfless act that humans were given medals for.

"I have David's wedding ring," she began. "I swore I'd never take it off, but perhaps now is the best time there'll ever be. If it went on one of your hands, and you melted it into the pool gates with you, it would be as if David got his final wish, and helped save us all from a disaster. I couldn't think of a better tribute to him."

"I can do that," he replied, and held out his hand. Emma slipped the ring on one of his fingers, but it wouldn't fit. She smiled and slid it on the smallest finger of the half-man in the passenger seat.

"Perfect," she said. "If rather different circumstances from the first time I did that."

They looked at each other again.

"I have to go now," he said.

"I know." Emma replied. "And thank-you Jed."

With a last glance that Emma could have sworn contained a smile, he opened the door and pulled himself out of the car and onto the road. It seemed strange to her that a last goodbye had passed so soon. As agreed, she drove off straightaway in case anyone was around, as if she'd only stopped in the lay-by to check her phone. But there was no one.

He pulled himself onto the verge quickly, and then assessed the gradient and nature of the river bank. It was full of bushes and clumps of taller grass to hold on to, so he scaled the drop easily.

He rolled into the river like a diver immersing themselves in the sea. The water felt only moderately cold through the sensors in his skin covering, and the favourable downstream current helped his momentum, as he made his way down the channel towards the Meadowpitch complex. Hands digging into the pebbles and earth to find grip and leverage, he moved forward with a sideways yaw like a clockwork shark.

With no need to surface to breathe, he could make discreet and steady progress along the riverbed. The recent rainfall had swelled the river's volume, which helped to keep him submerged. Even so, he stayed closer to the eastern bank, where there were more places to shelter if anything went wrong.

He navigated his way around rocks that broke the surface, and then went carefully around a small weir with several stretches of turbulent water, staying as close to the bank as he could to avoid the cascades. Eventually he arrived at the site of the overhead gantry that spanned the riverbanks, and continued across into the complex. He had to climb the support column carefully, knowing that one slip would mean disaster. Pulling himself upwards felt unusual, because when switching grip he had to counteract the swing to the opposite direction to where he wanted to go, without his legs to stabilise the natural roll of his upper body. But he improvised, and got the hang of the rhythm required to make better progress.

With considerable effort and energy use, he got to the top of the column, and looked around him from his vantage point. Apart from the movement of the odd night shift worker and a few security staff looking to be seen doing their duty, there seemed few people around. Along the gantry were the bodies of several dead seagulls, probably irradiated, he thought, after dropping into the pool to drink without realising the dangers of the water until too late. He noticed there was no roof on it, and that visiting birds could spread radioactive materials into the countryside before they died. One lay not far from him, tufts of feathers missing and blood oozing slowly out of open wounds.

He reasoned that a direct drop, from the gantry into the containment pool, was the safest way of ensuring he wouldn't sustain any more damage. So when he was two-thirds of the way over it, he paused and looked around below him. There were no staff nearby. He could do nothing about the noise of the splash, except hope it didn't raise alarms. It was possible that it would be picked up by remote microphones and cameras, so he would just have to hope that these were going to be disabled very soon by the hackers, or that the monitoring staff would be half-asleep.

Timing was everything. Too soon, and he might be discovered, in which case his self-destruct sequence would take care of it, and they'd just recover a heap of smouldering molten metal. Too late, and the sabotage would take effect so quickly he might find the time for his intervention had passed.

Then he noticed something. One by one, the security lights were turning off. He heard some chain-driven mechanical shutters being closed noisily in the distance. It was starting. The workers had no idea what was about to happen. He took one last look around him, then pushed himself off the edge of the gantry, free-falling into the radioactive pool with a dull splash. For a moment, his sensors were overloaded with details about the water temperature, pressure and radioactive contents, but as none of this mattered now he shut them off.

He sank easily to the lower levels with his weight, and then pulled himself along towards the end where the sluice gates were. If he could prevent them from opening, then the rest of the destruction couldn't happen, and the workers would have time to declare an emergency and close everything down as best they could, while they waited for reinforcements from anywhere still able to function.

He had no information on what exactly was going on outside the pool, although the dim resonance of alarms and sirens sounding seemed to filter their way down to him in the leaden depths. He was wholly focused on blocking the opening mechanism, before that too was compromised. While methodically scooping his way forwards through the dimly glowing sludge at the bottom, he could feel parts of his artificial skin starting to blister and flake off, but this meant nothing to him as it was no longer needed.

Soon he reached the sluice gates, and that was as far as his existence was going to take him. The programming, the preparation, the journey through time, the accidental arrival in the tree, and the chance meeting with the boy and the woman, had all come to this.

A cage surrounded the gates, but the grilles were just wide enough to force himself through, although he noticed there wasn't enough room for what would have been the rest of his body. As he looked down, he saw through the murky water that the intense radiation had by now melted off all of his skin covering, leaving only the metallic casings underneath.

He placed his hands on the gates either side of the divide, and began his self-destruct sequence. The hands ignited and started to burn him into position, as the water sent superheated bubbles cascading up to the surface. There was still no one around to notice, as all the guards were frantically chasing around in panic mode, with confused and conflicting messages emerging from the torment in their headsets. As his fingers melted themselves on to the gates, David's wedding ring glowed, like a lucky horseshoe fresh from a forge, before dimming. It became just another part of the horizontal bracing, made up of his hands and arms, for the main infilling weld that the rest of his body would provide. Becoming the welding seam was the whole purpose of his existence now, as it always had been. The sound of the name 'Jed' passed through his silicon memory and then disappeared.

Having secured his position, his main torso started to heat up from the base, the improvised lower seal crackling in the heat like randomly spitting oil from a Sunday roast in a blistering oven. Soon the heat was up to his chest and his melting torso was steadily blocking up the gap and welding the gates shut. All of this he monitored closely. His mission would be accomplished soon. He was almost at the end, with just his head and neck remaining.

Pressing his face to the top of the gates, he could feel the heat rise through the last of his metallic vertebrae, fusing them together before dissolving them into metallurgic lava. The water all around him was sizzling and boiling, but there were no longer any functioning cameras to record it. Closedown was coming soon.

The front of his face stickily dissolved into the gap at the top of the gates, and he could feel the sensors in his nose disintegrate. Then the redness entered into his brain circuits, and he was subsumed in a fiery orange glow that turned a raging blue, as his skull grew hotter and hotter still, and he melted further into the gap. A fleeting image of a boy and a woman running towards a smouldering tree came and went. As the last of his head was fusing into place, a pulse of light shone brightly from it, illuminating the depths like a submersible's searchlight. And then it all went dark again, and he had become part of the gates, now secured by every atom of the cooling steel crucifix which clenched them together as one.

The signal to open them came through strongly, exactly as encoded in the malicious hack, but the tenaciously gripped gates resisted. Again and again the signal tried to make the connection, until the motor circuits burned out, and the hack was done. The gates remained triumphantly shut. There would be no meltdown, no explosion, no deadly, life-destroying radioactive cloud over northern Europe. His work was finished, and so was he.

The Third Shipwreck

The two men in the blue uniforms looked relaxed and entered the room, one after the other, with a calm authority. They sat down on the chairs waiting for them. They looked at each other, then at the man in front of them at the table, and nodded. It was time to start the debriefing.

"Just tell us everything you can remember. There's no rush. The more detail, the more you can help us picture what happened," said the man who had entered first, his confident presence reassuring and supportive.

"And from the beginning too, so we get things in the right order. We want to put all the pieces in place like a jigsaw. From what we've heard about it already, it's quite a story," the man who had entered second chimed in, before settling back in his chair. He was not expecting a short session.

The man at the table before them smiled. At last, he would get another chance to explain what had happened, with people he could trust. They were much younger than him, of course, but wasn't everyone these days?

"*Ships and shipwrecks,*" he began. "*My life has revolved around them both. When I left the navy, about a year after Queen Victoria's coronation, I worked for Major-General Charles Pasley's team, who were salvaging cannons from the Royal George. It had sunk about fifty years previously at Spithead in one of the biggest naval disasters in British history.*"

The two visitors exchanged a quizzical glance after the mention of him working in the reign of Queen Victoria. This was going to be quite a tale. The speaker went on.

"*We used the Deane brothers' helmets at first, but found they could have dangerous leaks if you bent over too far. Siebe's suits and helmets were the best. And what a time we had. Once we used so much gunpowder to blow apart the wreck, windows were broken by the blast across the water in Portsmouth!*"

The listeners nodded to each other. This was someone who had all the facts at his fingertips. It sounded like everything had happened too long ago, but they were expecting that. This just intrigued them further, so they raised no objection for now. He continued.

"*While on leave I visited Gloucester to see the cathedral where, luckily, I met my eventual fiancée, Eliza. She showed me a pamphlet she'd been given the previous day, about how our natural liberty was being restrained by unfair laws. After a discussion, we realised we shared many views. We both had spent much of our adult lives reading whatever we could get our hands on, and going to talks on all manner of subjects. Then we attended a meeting together, in about April of eighteen forty-two, it* must have been."

The other men exchanged another glance at the mention of the date of the meeting, but still said nothing. The speaker clearly believed every word he was saying.

"*It was at the Cheltenham Mechanics' Institute, and given by George Holyoake. He said the country was too poor to pay twenty million pounds a year towards the church. So as religion was too expensive, he suggested putting God and the clergy on half-pay to save money. That proposal earned him six months in Gloucester Gaol. After that, we resolved to keep our real views and opinions to each other, as we agreed with Holyoake's ideas for social progress.*

I left Pasley's service after his salvage operation had ended, and he generously gave me my diving suit as a reward for my services. Eventually, I secured a position for several years at a new diving school run by the Royal Navy, and based at HMS Excellent on Whale Island. Eliza went with me, and gathered in time an impressive collection of books and pamphlets on the rights of women, an issue I wholeheartedly supported.

However, we realised London was really the place to be, to keep up with the leading ideas of the day, and to live there we would need more money than I could earn at the diving school. When the chance to join a lucrative voyage came up, we decided it would best for me to take it, even if it meant a separation of a year or two. The opportunity had come about when I'd met the scientist Alfred Wallace, through his friend Henry Bates, who had suggested they could benefit from a diver on their expedition to explore the Amazon River. They were going to search for new species of fish and crustaceans. I had long been an admirer of the work of Doctor Darwin, whose books and poetry had engrossed me for countless hours. The chance to work with Wallace, who had similar interests to the doctor, was too good to turn down.

Eliza had relatives in London who needed a governess, and so she could support herself that way. The earnings from the expedition would pay for our marriage, which we both desperately wanted as we had become very close, and allow us to settle in the capital at last. We both agreed the sacrifice of our being apart for a while would be worth it. Then we could have the rest of our lives together, and we still felt young enough to see it all through.

After an emotional farewell to Eliza, we left for the Amazon on the Mischief on the twenty-sixth of April, eighteen forty-eight, from Liverpool, just two days after we had celebrated her birthday, which she described to me as the happiest day of her life, given our promises to each other. The voyage went well, although I discovered it took longer to develop my sea legs in the open ocean. I was mightily relieved to enter the port of Pará in Brazil just over a month later.

The explorations made much progress early on. Wallace was convinced that having a diver gave us an advantage over the expeditions by other Europeans who, like us, wanted to find specimens of new species to catalogue and sell back in London. However, he had the additional aim of finding evidence for transmutation, and I had many conversations with him and Bates about that when the weather was inclement for foraging or diving.

Wallace had taken two prized books with him, which he allowed me to read. Chambers' Vestiges of the Natural History of Creation and Edwards' A Voyage Up The River Amazon absorbed my leisure for many hours. He was also an accomplished artist, and he would draw countless pictures of what we found, a collection that would no doubt be invaluable back home.

I helped catch many examples of river tortoises of different species, and Wallace told me he was very proud of those. He said transmutation could be proved by how their bodies changed, according to the different types of water they lived in.

Once I trapped a type of royal peacock bass, near a jungle overhang, that was one of the biggest fish we had ever seen, and must have weighed over thirty pounds. Fish provided us with much needed nourishment, and we cooked different species of piranha and catfish almost every evening.

I particularly enjoyed one meal, where we gutted and cooked a monstrous fish with a huge and vicious mouth, which had bitten my leg so hard it had got through one of the legs of my diving suit, leaving me with a half-ring of teeth marks just below my left knee. That feast was sweet revenge indeed. I kept its jaw bones as a somewhat morbid souvenir, but I knew one day I would enjoy showing them to Eliza, along with the sizeable scars I would retain as a souvenir of the encounter!

When Bates and Wallace split up to cover more ground I went with Wallace, and we charted much of the Rio Negro in considerable detail. The more differences in species I saw, the more I agreed with Wallace's ideas on transmutation. Creatures changing for the better would have a greater chance of survival, and naturally outlast others who stayed the same. If only he could have met Doctor Darwin and discussed his theories with him!

But he also believed in an immortal spirit, which I did not. I had seen too many divers lost in accidents, and thought death simply a brutal and all-conquering fact. For that reason, I stayed well away from strange currents and the whirlpools underneath waterfalls, that could draw a helmeted diver to a suffocating doom.

Wallace respected the local inhabitants, and drew on their knowledge of the area. The Tukano and Arawak were our allies, and the elderly ex-slave Isidoro proved an invaluable guide. He was a man whose closeness to nature I came to respect as much as the proud learning of any well-dressed man in South Kensington. Wallace thought that men differed solely by opportunity, not any innate superiority, and on that we wholly concurred.

Our leader excelled in his role and purpose, and our team was even joined by his younger brother, Edward, who soon mastered the hand-cranking of the small pump on the river raft that sent my air supply down to me. Sadly, Edward did not survive a bout of yellow fever, and he passed away at far too young an age. That was the start of the undoing of the expedition.

The exhausting demands of living next to the jungle debilitated Wallace, despite the generous hospitality of our acquaintances in their huts. He was still grieving the loss of his brother, and after being plagued with ill health, we decided returning home was the only wise choice left. With heavy hearts we returned downriver to the coast.

We had chartered cabins on a brig, the Helen, for the voyage and for several days we loaded it with our prime specimens and enough supplies for the journey. I settled into my cabin well and for the first few days was pleased at the absence of sickness, my sea legs returning with commendable haste. Wallace continued to make drawings of some of the specimens he had brought with him, so they were ready to publish when we returned to our home shores.

The days went past slowly but steadily, and my thoughts began to revolve around my future life with Eliza. She had managed to send a few letters, which had been ferried up to where we had been on several occasions, so I was aware the role of governess had suited her well and she was being amply rewarded for all her efforts. She had informed me that the Navy was considering opening another diving school, in a spare shipbuilding yard at Deptford in London, and would need a new instructor, a position for which I would surely apply. Our separation would soon be coming to an end, and my heart was bubbling up with anticipation.

On the morning of the sixth of August, as I had not used my equipment in a long while, I decided to go down into the hold to scrutinise it, as mould was the bane of a diver's life, and the suit had to be kept away from any damp when it was not in regular use.

As I neared the section where my equipment was secured, I could smell something acrid in the air, and turning a corner saw flames. Immediately, I shouted out to sound the alarm and grabbed the nearest fire bell, which I rang with vigour for several five-second intervals, as was the custom for emergencies. I could hear the consternation arise above me on deck, but as I ran back I committed a foolish error, and over-estimated the headroom to the stairs. My forehead collided with the entrance lintel, delivering to my head a prodigious blow. I staggered backwards and fell into the nearest doorway, collapsing in the room alongside the large trunk full of my diving apparatus.

When I came to, after I know not how long, the ship was badly listing, and bitter, softly swirling smoke had settled on the ceiling above me like an ominously low cloud of thickening stratus. My clothes were wet, and I realised the cabin was flooding and the ship was sinking. It was then that I became aware of the heat, and I could hear the noises of timber cracking and spitting like spiteful logs at a Viking funeral.

I looked out the porthole, and saw several rowing boats already some distance away. I tried calling but knew, even if they had heard me, they would have been risking all their rescued passengers and crew to try and save me, as the ship could overturn and sink at any moment.

This bad luck might have sent me on my way to a briny burial, but I had a fortuitous inspiration. I opened the trunk and began to dress in my suit as quickly as I could, trying to control the desperation that would otherwise outpace the rising waters. When I was at last ready to secure my helmet, they had risen inside the cabin to my waist. I had a small breathing canister with a tube attached for air, that might afford me sufficient time to escape the giant oak-beamed coffin that the Helen was fast becoming.

With the air supply attached, I slowly advanced to the doorway, just as the ship keeled over to starboard with a wrenching strain that shuddered the planking under my hefty boots. As I made my *way through the opening, the waters surged and flooded the rest of the cabin, almost carrying me with them, but I was determined to reach the slanting stairway ahead. I pulled my way through it as if exiting a subterranean tunnel, and emerged out of the other side just as the ship rolled onto its back, the sea extinguishing the fires with a mighty onrush. I found myself submerged under the deck of the Helen, as if the globe itself had turned turtle, and displaced the summer sky with an unfathomable darkness.*

Wary of the deadly vortexes of sinking ships, that were known to drag overboard sailors down to their doom, I attempted to grasp my way across to the quarter deck, but as I reached it I could feel the last remnants of the Helen's hold on the surface loosen and let slip. The bow tipped down into a deadly descent, dragging the rest of the ship with it. I pushed myself away into more open waters, but it was too late. I was upended, and lost all sense of up or down. I knew in my heart that I was being dragged to the depths below, and that the pressure would soon overwhelm even my beloved suit and helmet, which had kept me safe through many an adventure since I had first used them at Spithead.

As the depth increased, and the pressure mounted, I found it harder and harder to breathe, until all I could manage was the slight panting of an exhausted dog. All around was an opaque void, and soon the enveloping darkness came inside my helmet and my skull, and I said my farewells to the world and hoped Eliza would forgive me. I expected only death."

The first man stood up and puffed out his cheeks with an audible sigh, as if to say this was a whole lot of drama for a Wednesday afternoon. He leaned against a wall, stretched out his arms, and then gestured to the speaker to carry on, which he promptly did.

"You can imagine my dumbfounded astonishment that I did not actually pass away. Instead, I awoke in the bowels of another

vessel, made of steel of some kind, and unlike any ship I had ever seen before. I was strapped to a bunk with several large belts, and wearing some garments of a linen-like cloth. I blinked to more fully awaken my eyes, in case I was really at the bottom of the ocean, and hallucinating away my final moments. But how was I dry? Where was my suit? And were the rest of the crew still in their lifeboats and safe on the seas above me?

Raising my head, I looked around and could see the shapes of people making their way towards me, as if they were floating in the ether. They were similarly dressed, in what looked like some form of casual uniform, and with not a hint of breathing equipment in sight. I was familiar with diving bells and such like, but never at this depth. And how were they floating, unbound by the chains of gravity?

The people came to me and when they spoke, my world turned upside down again just as surely as if I was back in the Helen and capsizing once more. They could understand me and I them, and I learned things that I would scarcely have believed, had I not heard them myself from the occupants of the metal ship, who had saved my life.

My rescuers were 'monitors,' as they called themselves, from another unimaginably distant world. They had observed events on our planet over a number of years, becoming accustomed to our ways of speaking, and lived off their own resources aboard the ship. They kept themselves to themselves unless an emergency arose, such as my near-drowning, in which case their intervention was permitted.

They had followed Wallace's expedition because they saw transmutation as a sign of how far a civilisation had progressed in the quest for knowledge. They had not anticipated the Helen's disastrous fate, and were merely shadowing it under the surface while recording the songs of whales. Apparently whale song amounted to a language that could traverse great distances, and they were trying to decipher it.

They were not able to prevent the Helen sinking, but they did see me emerge from the descending hull as they were tracking the ship underwater, and so were able to effect a rescue through some sort of grappling force, which pulled me to the safety of their vessel.

However, I was soon doubly astonished, as when I was unbelted I also floated up into the space around me. Words cannot describe this confutation of Newton's Laws of Gravity, or the feeling of nausea that possessed me as surely as if I was back on the Mischief in the midst of a tempest. The primal notions of up and down had been cast adrift, and I could somersault as easily as any circus performer, but without needing to find my feet afterwards. Indeed, my feet seemed to have lost their original purpose in life altogether, and to have been replaced by my hands grabbing holds to propel me along, in a truly unholy form of locomotion!

My remaining anchor to the world, as I had known it, was then also thrown overboard, for I was taken to a porthole from which I could see our huge planet unimaginable fathoms beneath me, where all its people, and Wallace and the other survivors in their lifeboats, and my dear Eliza, probably engaged in reading lessons or suchlike for her charges, ever so distantly dwelled. The globe revolved into night below, and there were pinpricks of light where cities shone into the darkness. Then, it revolved into day again, and with unseemly haste, until I realised that this was just the effect of our vessel flying over it at speed, and a day down there still had its full twenty and four hours. Everything seemed terrifyingly out of reach, and I felt doubly nauseous for an instant. I looked across in amazement at my rescuers, who explained themselves further.

After their monitoring of Earth was concluded, the travellers informed me, they would return to their home planet, which cir-

*cled round a distant star just visible in our night sky, and report
back on what they had found. And they wished me to accompany
them."*

The second man shuffled in his chair a little, and then spoke.

"That would have been a very long way away, wouldn't it?
I've heard it could take years to get someplace else in the galaxy."

"Yes," agreed the first. "You would need plenty of hobbies to
get through that journey! And you'd sure need to be able to get
on with your crewmates."

They exchanged smiles.

"But what about the girl you left behind?" the seated man
enquired. "If she was such a good prospect, why did you leave
her in the lurch, after you'd been saved from drowning by the
...?"

"Monitors," the first man interjected with a grin and a nod,
as if congratulating himself for concentrating all the way so far.

The speaker's confident air dissipated and he looked embarrassed and uncomfortable.

*"I had to make the biggest decision of my life at this point. I
suspected their planet would be a long distance away. But I had
thought that I would be able to return and resume our relationship, with our future made from the tales I could tell. I imagined
myself as some sort of celebrated orator, I suppose, speaking at
meetings much as Holyoake had."*

His face contorted slightly, and his eyes filled with the tears
from a bitter regret, as though he was forcing himself to swallow
a slice of rancid lemon.

*"I was not thinking clearly. Perhaps the deep descent alongside
the wrecked Helen had scrambled my brains somewhat. I had
known divers, starved of oxygen, who came to the surface like
punch-drunk pugilists and never regained their former selves. I
will never understand why I failed to consider that Eliza would*

have had word from Wallace that I was missing at sea, and what that would have done to her.

But in truth, I had no real idea of how long I would be away for. I did not discover that until it was too late. I should have enquired further before the voyage started, but did not. It is a regret I will take to the grave. Instead, I acquiesced, overwhelmed by events and my rescue, and chose a future course I would unwittingly steer alone."

The seated man made a gesture with upturned hands as if to say, 'Well, that's life.' The speaker nodded slowly, and then continued.

"To prepare for the travel through space, I was enclosed in a vertical cylinder behind robust doors that locked firmly shut. I felt trapped and queasy, as though something exceedingly dangerous was about to happen. I could feel some type of valve being opened and an increasing pressure in my ears, as a fluid started to flood into the cylinder, pressurising the remaining air, which then seeped out of a valve above the top of my head. Becoming steadily immersed in a strange-smelling liquid, slightly reminiscent of the kind embalmers use, I thought to forestall the inevitable end of drowning for as long as possible. I filled my lungs with the remaining air, as if I was about to do a long dive into the sea unaided. I had been forewarned of the general process, but had presumed some means of breathing air was built in to the contraption.

For a moment I wondered at the deception and cruelty of my captors. They appeared to have rescued me only in order to condemn me, perhaps to some damned drowning sacrifice to bless the journey ahead. But as the unfamiliar fluid filled the last spaces around my chin, it felt like it was already seeping into my body through my skin. The desire to hold my breath disappeared, like the air itself, and I experienced an unlikely onset of calm.

When the liquid went past my mouth and nose, you would expect me to have panicked and have confronted my own demise at any second, but not at all. It just entered my throat and descended into my lungs as if it was soothing my senses all the way down. Far from choking or spluttering with the desperation of drowning, I experienced the deepest state of relaxation I had ever known, as though my mind was becoming unchained from my body and could float around at will.

Looking around me, I could no longer make out the interior of the strange ship through the glass eyeholes of the cylinder that I was entombed in, as my vision seemed to draw in upon itself. But I now felt reassured that my rescuers bore me no ill will.

I know not how much time passed in this strange state. I had pleasant dreams of Eliza and talked to her often around the kitchen table. Visions of the countryside around my childhood home came before me, where I would play with the dogs in the field before taking my turn at feeding the animals. Thoughts of money or work had I none, except for when I was floating under the waves and seeing majestic beings swimming by, or back in the Amazon searching for creatures yet to be identified by Wallace.

I felt no hunger or pain. Indeed, I remember thinking on one occasion that I felt nothing at all. There were no sensations, just thoughts passing through me like trains in a station, going every way they fancied, and it was not unpleasant. I imagined that this must be how it would feel to be under laudanum or suchlike. Were it not for my distinct memory of the monitors placing me in the cylinder, I might have thought that I had drowned aboard the Helen as it sank, with it taking me down to share its watery grave after all.

I no longer remembered the difference between sleep and wakefulness. Of course, there was no night or day, but nor was there any sense of waking from a restful absence. I simply felt I was always conscious, and was unaware of when I wasn't.

Eventually I could hear noises outside the cylinder, and this brought me fully back to myself after I know not how many days or weeks, and I realised I had lost all sense of time itself. Then the fluid started to drain from the cylinder, and was replaced by a sweet smelling warm air, which was not disagreeable either. As my lungs emptied out any remaining fluid, I half expected a choking or coughing reflex, but there wasn't one, as the fluid seemed to evaporate into the air without a trace.

When I raised my hands to my face it felt dry. It was as if I had long been breathing air from the freshest source, and had had no encounter with moisture of any degree. Nor had my beard grown, leaving me with the same spiky stubble I had promised myself to shave later in that fateful day on the Helen. Similarly, my body felt dry, and I felt no compulsion to relieve myself, or any desire to plunge into a stream or waterfall in nature to clear out my extremities."

At this point, a slight clearing of the throat led to him coughing, and he looked up with slightly watering eyes as the first man offered him a drink from a cup already in the room. The speaker took it to his lips and emptied it eagerly, for the talking had made him thirsty.

"You were telling us about when you came out of the cylinder," the second man said, slowly and encouragingly, and then moved his hand as if to say keep it rolling.

"Yes, the cylinder. When the doors opened, I came out of it as free of moisture as a snake in a desert. They helped me put on a robe and I floated, aware this time of how peculiar it felt, to a viewing window. I had arrived above another planet, which in no way resembled the home world I had glimpsed from above before entering that cylinder of dreams. There were docking jetties for

their space vessels, which were tended by cables and hoses of all manner of sizes and lengths, no doubt replenishing supplies after long voyages.

I counted at least twelve sizeable ships in the docks, each on a scale incomparably vaster than HMS Indus, the only large warship I'd ever seen up close. Further to the left, I could see spinning steel hoops of vast diameters, revolving as effortlessly as wheels on a penny-farthing bicycle. To my right, there were immense mirror-like structures that shone with the light from their sun like they were on fire.

Soon I was boarded on a type of launch craft that was to go to the planet. I wondered if I might meet a king or other imperious ruler, but after a short ride through the skies, at first surrounded by an intense fire I could see through a small porthole – which I had been warned to expect – we landed at another dock and disembarked, with no grand reception, as if the arrival of creatures like me had happened before.

I was led to another carriage, with no means of propulsion I could determine, and which released neither smoke nor steam into the air. Our group sat down and another journey began. The carriage was enclosed in glass, so I could see our route reveal itself as we progressed. Buildings gained in height, until I could no longer determine where they ended and the sky began.

All around, other flying carriages whirred in the air like bees amassing nectar and returning to their hives. I was so taken with the scene that it took me a good while to realise that there was no coachman in any of them, or indeed in ours. Before long, we arrived at a mansion of many floors, which seemed to be at the heart of the city, and gleamed in glinting bronze.

I was escorted to a lifting cage which travelled up the side of the building, so that you could see the ground give way beneath you. Would that a device like this had been available in the opposite direction for the descent to the St George! I could see sunlight beaming in from above, and realised I was probably quite some way distant from home. Doctor Darwin had written of there being many stars in the heavens, and I realised this planet must be orbiting another of them.

Disembarking the lift, we progressed to a grand room where pictures played on enormous screens like moving heliographs, but in such vivid colours that you could almost step inside them and think them real. I was led onto what looked like a stage, and sat in a group of chairs apparently set out to receive our party of travellers from the heavens. I feared I was being presented like a human oddity in a travelling circus, but as an audience arrived and took their seats, I realised I was more like a guest of honour at a scientists' symposium, and many proceeded to ask questions about my life and the world I came from.

My fellow travellers, as I called them, ably translated for me, as they seemed to have as good a grasp of the Queen's English as any person I had encountered at home. The whole event lasted some hours, and reminded me of a lecture on electricity by Faraday I had seen once at the Royal Institution in London, while on leave from the navy diving school, which had finished with long discussions of the audience's questions. It was there I had first met Sir George Cayley, who had already designed and flown a gliding machine. He had moved on to a design for an aerial carriage, and was considering how to power such a contraption from Faraday's force of electricity, his own designs for a hot air engine proving too heavy in theory to get it off the ground, and I related all this to the inquisitive attendees.

Many other topics were discussed, and I enlightened them further about the ideas of Doctor Darwin and others. They were pleased we had come so far as to understand transmutation as the survival of the strongest, following our development from prior species.

His drawings for a rocket engine drew significant interest, and another traveller wondered if it would spur a revolution in industry in my nation, possibly leading to the Queen forming a new regiment of the empire above the very heads of her subjects. Doctor Darwin's thoughts on star formation and decay were also thought to be ahead of their time. The chairman of the symposium then said he was one the greatest visionaries the symposium had heard of from any planet. Praise indeed for the good doctor!

I told them I regretted that Wallace had never been able to meet him, as I am sure they would have had many ideas in common. I then gave an account of my conversations with Wallace about transmutation. Many agreed that he was likely to become one of the most influential thinkers of the next decades back on Earth, and one of the other travellers said he was looking forward to finding out.

It was at this point that I began to realise the real purpose of my voyage there. Apparently, I was a living witness to the state of ideas on our planet, which the monitors were reporting back on. My testimony preceded a general discussion as to how these might develop, and there was to be a second visit to assess this progress.

After the event was over, I was escorted to another part of the building where I partook in a sumptuous banquet with the other fellows. I had the chance to thank particularly the traveller who had rescued me and my equipment from the sinking Helen. It was he who had been delegated with explaining what lay ahead of me, and I learned what this was with an open mouth and a considerable degree of trepidation.

Jevosa, as he told me he was so named, explained that I was only one of many witnesses that they secured every year from other planets, a process that had been going on for centuries. The race *on Zekrotia, as they called their own planet, saw themselves as custodians of the history of many other worlds, akin to a galactic Library of Alexandria. As they amassed these histories, they also compared them, and each planet visited would have at least one further follow-up trip to determine which luminaries had advanced the civilisation the most, and which empires had risen and fallen, and why.*

They were particularly interested in civilisations at the stage of exploring transmutation, and which were close to developing flight and then space travel. I agreed with Jervosa that Sir George Cayley's flying machines at the turn of the century, together with Doctor Darwin's design for a rocket engine, could bring forth enormous changes, even in the short time we had been away, given the resources the Empire could command when necessary."

The second man shuffled in his seat uncomfortably, as if this talk of flying machines and rockets was somehow all from the wrong age. He looked over at the first man, who shrugged his shoulders, and the speaker carried on regardless.

"Then Jevosa revealed the nature of the time that had passed during our voyage, and that we had travelled a great distance at an enormous velocity, easily approaching the speed of light. I gasped, as Bradley had calculated a value for this, which I remembered as a time of just over eight minutes for sunlight to travel the distance between the Earth and the Sun. As we had sustained a speed greater than that for untold months or even years, we must therefore be much further away than I had ever imagined. He nodded and said yes, Bradley's figure was a good approximation, and we had indeed been travelling for years. But there was something else that had occurred as a result.

Apparently, time would have passed differently for those we left behind on Earth. We had established Greenwich as the start of ship time for longitude, since the year before the Mischief set sail, so

I did not understand at first why there was no longer a universal duration pertaining to the heavens. Jevosa explained that, as we had travelled so quickly, our experience of temporality had been different. Although we wouldn't be able to feel any divergence, our ship time was actually going by far more slowly in relation to the people left at home.

As the journeys were still very long, the crews slept through them in the cylinders, which preserved their strength and vigour, and I was reminded of hibernating bears emerging in the spring after passing a hard winter in a place of shelter, and being unaware of how far they had travelled around the sun while asleep. But how far had we voyaged? And how much time would have passed at home? The questions came pouring out of me like wastewater from a bilge pump, and Jevosa was hard-pressed to keep up with answers.

But then one question emerged to tower over the others like a calamitous waterspout. It was about Eliza, and her lifespan, and my heart sunk to the bottom of my chest as he answered it. He put his hand on my shoulder, and consoled me that she would have been dead of old age by many decades already, as over half a century would have passed on Earth for each leg of our monumental excursion. I felt myself welling up with sorrow, as if the fluid in the cylinder was permeating me once again, but allowed him to finish.

He also admitted that the formation of each monitor team on their planet was an emotional experience, because each would know that this Disparate Chronometry, as they called it, would occur during the voyage, and so they would lose contact forever with their friends and families as the decades mounted in their absence. There was no one for them to come back to, which was why no one had waited to greet them on arrival. Everyone they had ever known had long since passed away.

However, their society had been stable for millennia, which allowed them to have continuity through the meetings of the returning travellers. Records of first visits to planets were scrupulously kept, which were then compared to the results of the second visits. This process could take hundreds of Zekrotia years for each of the planets they studied. The monitors saw time over centuries, not individual lifetimes, and the complete absence of political conflict or revolution enabled that to be so.

This scale of temporality and loss was becoming rather straining at this point, so I asked for privacy for a good while and retired to the room I had been allocated for the night. My thoughts kept returning to some lines of Dickens, about wearing a chain forged of bad decisions in life, decisions which had been made through our own free will. Across the vast distance of space, and over the many, many years, I would have to bear the chain of guilt for my failure to determine how long I would be absent from my planet, and from my dear Eliza.

She would have died of old age decades ago, never knowing that I survived the sinking of the Helen. I wondered if she ever found another suitor more loyal than I. Bitter regret consumed my very being, and I drifted off to a sleep of fits and starts. Images of Eliza transforming into an old woman in my still youthful arms, while I tried to somehow comfort her, plagued my dreams.

Up until then I had thought myself a good man, and I was shocked to realise that, to the contrary, I had not been. The chain of regrets was heavy indeed, and it was mine alone to bear. My hosts had not told me all that I should have known before our departure, but nor had I asked them the right questions, and the first of those should have concerned Eliza."

The first man leaned back against the wall and carefully drew a handkerchief from his pocket to clear his nose. He shook his head slowly as if in sympathy. The debrief continued.

"The next morning Jevosa returned, and he again commiserated on the tragic consequences of Disparate Chronometry. He said that all their guests were given a choice, of whether to return to their home planet, or to remain there with them. I requested further evidence of the condition of those who had stayed, and he took me to yet another part of the building, which we accessed by moving walkways such that every step was multiplied many times over, and we could walk with an unseemly pace.

We arrived at an assortment of indoor gardens, where the strangest collection of creatures I had ever seen were resting, talking together or playing games unknown to me. How Wallace would have been enraptured by the scene! I knew not of other planets, except of my home and that of the travellers, but my imagination leapt at the thought of the countless other worlds that had been visited to assemble such a cluster of transported species. Indeed, I was reminded of Wallace's collection of animal specimens, which had presumably been lost with the Helen.

Although I could not fathom what any of the creatures were saying, I could see that not all had integrated well, and were seated alone, or wandering as if their ship's clock had lost its mounting and rolled overboard. They were sailors marooned in place and time, like secluded Robinson Crusoes who could never cast off from the islands in their heads.

My host confirmed with me that they were all from planets that had been monitored over the years, and whose societies had become aware of transmutation as the driver of progress and change in all forms of life. The choice, of staying on Zekrotia or returning home, was also being offered to me.

Wandering through the gardens, but unable to communicate with the others, I decided that adding myself to my hosts' collection was likely to be a long and lonely experience. I chose to return, for although it was to a planet with no one left in it that I would know, *it was still my home. I preferred to end my days alongside others of my kind, even as a pitifully haunted soul in the right place, but the wrong age.*

And so it was that I eventually found myself again in the strange cylinder, with the liquid that passed over my face and flowed into my body, bringing with it the dream state of wonder and reflection, which sobered only at the journey's end.

As the cylinder emptied once more, I felt a rising sense of anticipation about what the portholes would reveal this time. Perhaps the scene would be like the spaceports above Zekrotia, as many decades would have passed on Earth. I expected grand Empire vessels and flying shuttle boats to be flitting hither and thither like inquisitive dragonflies. I imagined my reception with the latest monarch, and meetings with the descendants of Bradley, Doctor Darwin, Holyoake, Cayley, and Wallace. How people would be astonished to learn that these names were now known in another corner of the heavens, unimaginably far away in distance and years!

I don't deny that my excitement at the prospect of a reception ceremony akin to that on Zekrotia got the better of me at first, and I put aside my sadness over Eliza until it returned to overwhelm me. All my family, friends and her, now lost some place in time that had gone for ever, as indeed for them had I."

"So you're back home now at this point in your travels," the seated man interrupted. "I just want to be clear on that."

The speaker nodded, before continuing again.

"I was helped out of the cylinder, and was pleased to see Jevosa again. Yet all apparently was not well. Or rather, nothing had developed as expected. He informed me that they had arrived some days previously, but had left me in the cylinder a little longer while they ascertained the true nature of what had happened in the intervening decades, presumably from monitoring telegraph

messages all around the world, or whatever types of signals had evolved in our absence, no doubt with the aid of difference engines of the sort envisioned by Babbage.

As I looked out of the portholes, I could see only the planet beneath me, which, I noticed this time, was encircled at the horizons by a pale blue aura. The vessels and docks I had expected to be all around us were nowhere to be seen. But when we circled the globe into night, I was shocked by the huge golden cobwebs of luminescence covering much of the planet. It seemed true night now dwelled but sparsely.

Jevosa unbelted himself from his post, and drifted across to where I was gazing outward. He agreed to summarise the changes and developments down below for me. Doctor Darwin was relatively unknown, despite the vindication of many of his scientific theories, which were now apparently labelled with terms like 'The Big Bang,' 'amino acids' and 'DNA'. Transmutation was now termed evolution, but the good doctor received no credit for inventing it. The Empire was dismantled and gone, and space itself was the province mainly of Americans, Russians and the Chinese. Several small space stations passed us by that were vastly inferior in size and function by comparison to the immense structures orbiting Zekrotia, and there had been no meaningful space travel, except for just half a dozen sightseeing trips to the moon and back in the previous century.

I was unsettled by the transformation. There was so much to take in. It was not the future I had imagined when I decided to return. Jevosa told me of many more things, of genocides, wars and colossal bombs, and atrocities by those wishing to unleash reigns of terror. But of the many images that I saw, one stuck out to me the most. It was a picture of an enormous ark in a field in the United States of America, seemingly commemorating Noah's escape from the Biblical flood. Straightaway, I knew that my return should begin with a visit to it. Given my loyalty to the theories of Doctor Darwin, the chance to scrutinise a monument opposing his ideas seemed a temptation of fate. I had to see it.

Jevosa agreed to disembark me there when they recommenced their observations, as long as I kept their presence a secret. There was to be no reception with the monarch in London, no speaking engagements, no Grand Tour of world capitals, for their work was not yet done and could not be compromised. I so burned with indignant curiosity, about the strange ark in the field, that I agreed.

Our landing vessel descended over an empty region of the northern Atlantic, to minimise the detection of our entry flames, and then we traversed a mighty distance above the waves, until we neared the coast of America on the east side. Overflying the city of Washington, I could make out the outline of the Capitol Hill building, and see the Washington Monument clearly, which Jevosa kindly pointed out, and which existed only as drawings and sketches as we had set sail for Pará all those years ago.

We halted outside of a town, and garments and supplies were procured, through money raised from the selling of artefacts collected from the travellers' first visit, in a procedure at a shop no doubt resembling a Saturday night at a pawnbroker's in Drury Lane. This allowed me to dress as a modern citizen and have the local currency of American dollars. I was advised that a British pound from when I left would now be worth not far short of a hundred dollars, so to be careful with the money I was using.

Then we had a short journey over huge forests, before arriving at our destination south of a town called Colcheth, where the ark was situated. We landed in a clearing surrounded by trees, and after a survey of the area confirmed we could not be seen, the hatch was opened. I said my goodbyes to the crew and to Jevosa, thanked them all for returning me safely, and wished them well for their next few years of monitoring, and for their final homeward journey.

It was then that I realised that because of Disparate Chronometry, as they had explained it, every person and creature that I had met when visiting their planet, including all the Robinson Crusoes, would likely have already passed on. Another brief wave of sorrow cascaded over me. As I looked back at the craft, the hatch closed, and it returned to its monitoring state of invisibility. I could not hear its levitation, but sensed a pulse of air pass over my body which surely indicated its departure. I presumed I was again alone, for the first time since my brief descent when dragged down by the sinking Helen."

"Home sweet home at last," the man leaning against the wall said, spacing out the words slightly to emphasise their significance to the speaker's tale. "So what happened next?"

"I headed a short distance to my right, where there was a small, paved road from the woods to the attraction. I proceeded up this road on foot for a good way, to the sound of the roar of innumerable vehicles thundering along a carriageway to the east, their engines providing a cacophony of droning and rumbling, as if many hulking hornets' nests were being rolled along the road at considerable speed.

On surmounting a small rise, I saw the reason for all the noise – never had I seen so many vehicles of different shapes, sizes and colours, all racing along the carriageway as if possessed by demons. Unlike the carriages on Zekrotia, they appeared to be limited to the road below, and flew not around the sky above. I strode parallel to this road on a grassy surface until I came upon the entrance to the centre, which gave preference to the many vehicles attending, such that an appreciably longer walk was necessary to the admissions desk.

After the exchange of a significant amount of currency, equivalent to almost four shillings in real money, I was at last able to mount a passenger vehicle, which seemed full of families eager to learn about Biblical history, and I noted how well dressed and presented they were.

Presently, we arrived at the exhibition centre, and after dismounting from the vehicle I proceeded through an archway with a simplistic rainbow painted on it. I was reminded of Wollaston's experiments, which proved that the colours were neither uniformly spread nor blended into each other. Once through this entrance I had my first glimpse of the ark.

It was enormous, although tiny in comparison with some of the vessels I'd seen docked above the atmosphere of Zekrotia. I couldn't help asking myself what Wallace would have thought. He was a spiritual man, but I don't know whether his faith would have allowed him to stomach the idea of a man building the ark at six hundred years old, and enduring through the rest of an extraordinary lifetime until nine hundred and fifty.

I wandered closer to the structure, which looked like it had been stranded by floodwaters receding as far back as the coast I had flown over with Jevosa. It towered over me, casting the deepest of shadows. I hesitated to call it a ship, as it was clear to me from the beginning that any vessel, of this size and shape, would have splintered into uncountable pieces on its first contact with storms such as the Mischief had encountered.

I made my way inside and looked around in increasing shock and disbelief. As I walked past an exhibit about men burning in Hell, accompanied with screaming and groaning from actors who appeared to be in hiding, as there were only sculptures of people to be seen, I couldn't help but become distressed. There was so much real knowledge in the world to be learned, and Holyoake had already provided the foundations for a new society without all these fears.

I looked around me at the accommodation the animals and other specimens were presumed to have been allocated, but there was no taking account of their different diets, or how all their excretions were to be evacuated to avoid a hideous stench. I thought to my own experience of confinement inside a capsule for many years during my star voyages, and was grateful for the protection the fluid had afforded me from the tribulations of ablutions. I shook my head in disbelief.

When I came across an exhibition of pictures of animals of different epochs playing together, and with children, my patience finally snapped. Doctor Darwin had spoken of the evolution of man from microscopic sea life to modern day creatures, through the new powers acquired over successive generations across millions of ages. He had even suggested that these successive generations would be found in different layers of rock, which would constitute monuments to the past of these beings. His insights had not been made welcome in this place. Indeed, it was claimed that the Earth was only a few thousands of years old – in fact, just a half dozen times or so older than Noah himself!

It all seemed terribly unfair, as though a miscreant sorcerer had collected all the knowledge from all the libraries in the world, jumbled it with a host of ancient fables, and unleashed a new Bedlam with the toxic concoction, in a ship built never to sail.

I left the exhibition, and soon found a talk going on in a half-empty hall next to the ark, in which the orator was claiming that the Flood was God's punishment for man going astray. I listened intently to his arguments, but when I got to the part where he said that millions of the many had deserved to be killed for the sins of the few, I felt a rage build inside me. All the mothers and children also sinners? Innocent women like my dear Eliza, condemned to drown in order to punish the faults of others? I could take no more!

I stood up and strode over to the presenter, who looked aghast at the interruption. Sensing movement from men in uniform at the back of the hall, who were striding towards me, I talked quickly to the audience.

'Listen to my words, for I have come far,' I began. 'I accompanied the great biologist Wallace on his journey to the Amazon and studied transmutation with him. I know it to be true, for I have seen how species adapted to changing rivers. And surely you must have heard of the great Doctor Darwin and his beliefs in transmutation, and his design for a rocket engine in the late eighteenth century?'

This last statement caused a pause in the audience's apparent hostility. The presenter looked across at me and smiled.

'So, you accompanied Wallace, you call evolution transmutation, and you think Darwin invented rockets – but in the eighteenth century?' the presenter asked me.

'Indeed so. Doctor Darwin was a prolific inventor and theorist. He also—' I began to reply.

'Charles Darwin was wrong on so many levels,' the presenter argued back, 'and never completed his medical studies, so was never a doctor. But at least give him his right time in hist—'

'Charles? Charles was just a voyager and illustrator,' I interrupted. 'He travelled to the Galapagos on The Beagle and produced a pleasing book of drawings, not long before I set sail with Wallace. No, I mean Erasmus, Charles' grandfather, who Charles never even met. Doctor Erasmus Darwin was one of England's greatest thinkers. Surely you have heard of him?'

'Oh, it's Erasmus now, is it?' the speaker noted. 'Has anyone here heard of Erasmus Darwin?' A chorus of laughter went around the hall.

'But he understood so many things you should have learned of. His name is even known on a faraway planet that I myself have visited,' I protested, forgetting my promise of discretion to the monitors in my anger.

'Oh, I see,' the speaker sneered at me. 'You mean you were abducted?'

There was a cacophony of derision, and I gazed around me, profoundly shaken by the hostility, until I was accosted by two officers of the attraction's constabulary, who held me firmly by the arms and led me towards the exit door of the hall.

'Erasmus!' I shouted loudly as I was being heaved forwards. 'Erasmus Darwin. Remember the name. The British Da Vinci! Look him up in your libraries. You will see he was right – and in seventeen ninety-six!'

I managed to shake off one of the guards just before the doors, and I turned about on one foot and shouted out Erasmus Darwin's most famous words before being manhandled outwards.

'The strongest and most active animal should propagate the species, which should thence become improved!' "

While relating these events he had become quite animated. The second man had closed his eyes to concentrate more deeply. The first man glanced over at the cup to suggest the speaker use it and he took a drink, before exhaling with relief at having managed to get through this part of his story. Then the speaker resumed.

"I was bundled away to the exit door, and discharged unceremoniously from the landlocked relic. Then they put me in a vehicle and drove me to the edge of the site, next to the place I had entered, and left me there. I looked across at the carriageway streaming with vehicles like a tributary of the Rio Grande, when we had funnelled the fish in it to better catch them. I resolved to take a stand at this place, but I was unsure of how best to proceed.

Walking along the edge of the road, I realised there was a footbridge of some kind across it further along, so I would not have to cross in front of the vehicles myself. Eventually I arrived at a general store where, from a courtyard in front of it, they also supplied a pungent-smelling propellant from brightly coloured pumps to power the vehicles. I asked there for devices to light a fire to warm myself in the night, and purchased several of them, a small amount of water, and what looked like ship's biscuits.

Returning to the museum entrance, I walked down the small road I had accessed from my point of disembarkation from the Zekrotian vessel. I then made off into the wooded areas to the west, circling behind the buildings carefully to avoid any further attention from the local constabulary.

After about half a mile, I crossed a small path and headed on west towards the setting sun, before turning north to the woods behind the main structure and waiting for dark. It was only then that I sensed my overwhelming hunger, so I ate all my biscuits and washed them down with some water. They were uncommonly sweet, as though laced with honey, but I felt better after having them.

Then I reflected on my position. It was not right that charlatans were exploiting the good nature of the innocent with such an un-feasible structure, which was packed full of tales from mankind's childhood, distortions about the younger Darwin, and not a mention of his more illustrious grandfather. I realised that, although I believed in Holyoake's notion of a civilised, free-thinking society, there might come a time when individuals were called to inter-vene more forcefully in events, and it was perhaps to this end that all my experiences had led. I resolved to set the ark afire, and expunge this aberration from the face of the Earth.

I waited for some time further, and when I was satisfied that the local constabulary had all retired for the night, I crept out of my hiding place and manoeuvred closer to the accursed vessel. Once inside, I made use of the straw that decorated many of the exhibits by setting it alight with the lighting devices I had purchased.

It did not take long to make my way through the charlatan ship, and I could see behind me the beginnings of a conflagration. It was as if the vessel was encountering the first soft flames of a righteous retribution, for all the distortions and falsehoods it was transporting on its maiden voyage to the underworld. I left the structure through a doorway on a higher level, proceeded over a walkway, and made my way across the open courtyard to the woods nearby.

It was a Nordic cremation of all the wrong turnings that had been made in society since my departure, and my tribute to all the luminaries who had gone before me, and so inspired me. The fire roared ever higher in the night sky, and I felt at peace. I sat on a fallen branch, near the edge of the woods I had emerged from, and watched over the scene. Flames escaped from their pagan pyre and leapt into the late evening sky, and the hull glowed with pulsating embers.

I lay on the ground next to the log and tilted my head such that it looked like the ark was upside down and pouring forth flames, like a waterfall from Hell, into the netherworld below. The air crackled, and the gentle breeze caressed the flanks as if blowing on them with breaths of purest oxygen. Had a fabled blacksmith been pumping his utmost with a mighty bellows, he could not have produced a hotter furnace in all of creation.

Fire brigadiers arrived in huge carriages with bright lights flashing, and sirens signalling the end of the world, but they were too late. All the separate fires I had started had long since taken hold, and merged into the unholy inferno. It was to be my third and final shipwreck, but on this occasion it was I who had been responsible for the wrecking. I leaned back on the log, shut my eyes, and fell swiftly asleep, exhausted by my travels and tribulations.

When I awoke, the wreck of the ark lay before my straining eyes in the aching dawn light. I had expected it to have only the remains of a keel and some parts of the hull, with the rest collapsed in a heap of ash and fire-blackened debris, but instead a huge stone carcass with squared towers had appeared from within, as if the wooden boat itself had been just a cruel deception, for such a ship could never have floated in even the most Biblical of floods.

As I looked around, I could see teams of constabulary exploring the area around the wreckage. It wasn't long before I was spotted, and several made their way over to me. I admitted to an act of, as I saw it, justifiable incendiarism, and I was taken to one of their vehicles and transported to the local station at Colcheth or some such place, for I was still much fatigued after all my travelling, and cared not.

After a not inconsiderable amount of questions, from a fair multitude of officers there, I was transported again to this place, and I have endeavoured to tell you both, as honestly and as accurately as I can, about all that has happened to me. I hope I have persuaded you of the veracity of my story, for it has accrued countless deaths in the making across the ages."

The speaker looked up from the place on the table where he had been staring while recounting the latter part of his tale. The second man appeared to have dozed off in his chair, and the first was making notes on a piece of paper he had pulled from a trouser pocket.

"Of course we're convinced," said the man leaning against the wall. "We couldn't pick holes in your tale if we tried. Hey Mitch," he called over to the dozing man in the seat. "Chow time is coming up soon."

Mitch opened his eyes and yawned satisfyingly. "Thanks Joe," he said.

"So what happens now?" the speaker asked.

"Oh, same old, same old. It's not like we have any say round here. And I've heard you'll be sticking around for quite a while. We'll probably drop by tomorrow as usual, either us or some of the other regulars, as you sure know how to fill an afternoon. Like we all say, in your room every day is Debriefing Day! But it's time for dinner now."

"Am I invited?"

"We all are, buddy," Mitch said.

They rose and escorted him to the door, where he paused for a moment. It had been good to recount what had happened to him once again. They walked into the hall and approached the serving bar, where food was dealt out on simple plates, and then collected their spoons to eat with. He never could fathom why they weren't allowed knives or forks, or why they all wore the same blue clothing.

After dinner he joined the other guests for the evening of moving pictures on a large glass screen that invited them into many worlds, all controlled by a host from a pointing wand in her hand. At the end of it, they were shown back to their rooms to retire for the night. The click of the key in the door confirmed that all would be well, and he curled up in his usual sleeping position under the bed, dragging the sheet on top of him, as he liked to do because it reminded him of his cabin in the Mischief.

He closed his right hand, enveloped it with his left, and brought them both up to his face. This helped him imagine being closer to his beloved Eliza, so dear to him despite the passage of so much hurtful time. He rubbed his nose softly against his left thumb, to remind himself of the feeling of touching their noses together, which had been a little tender ritual of theirs before parting.

"Goodnight Eliza."

"Goodnight Adam."

As he drifted off, he rubbed his left leg below the knee, where the crescent of scars from so long ago still itched on his skin from time to time, and all the lights in his head went out once again.

Don't Tell The Trees

S o far, not so good. Not good at all. Catastrophic, in fact.

The first colony had apparently been thriving, until a megaflare from their star had incinerated all living organisms on that side of the planet, where unfortunately the settlement had been located. Just half a day later – or earlier – and the base would have been shielded by billions of tons of rock. Very unlucky, Barbaroux thought.

The second group of colonisers had chosen a different system with a dimmer star, which they'd anticipated had millions of years of life left in it. They'd anticipated wrongly. Their sun had suffered an exponential core collapse, and the fusion process had switched to a low simmer within just a few years, which had doomed the life on its planets to a grasping chill. Unable to revive their rocket, which had been repurposed into the main power source for the primary base, they had slowly frozen to death when the rocket's spare thorium rods had been used up. The flight over their settlements revealed only graveyards encased in frost and ice.

The third group had seemed to fare much better with their planetary choice. Their sun was a stable, middle-aged star, and their planet, although fourth out in the system, was still warm enough to be comfortably habitable. But by the time the ship had arrived in orbit, it was nearly out of fuel, so the commander had decided to risk a landing despite sensor reports confirming native inhabitants. Unfortunately, the stone-age species who already lived there had not taken kindly to the arrival of humans.

The colonisers had the advantage of lightweight, devastating weaponry. But the locals had the numbers. Caring not for their own survival, waves of attackers slowly wore down the defenders of the emergency base, which had been set up around the landing vessels. Even an attrition rate of one to one hundred changed little, except to inexorably wear down the resistance of the colonisers one body at a time.

Eventually, a last stand had to be made. Groups of volunteer couples and families burrowed deeply away from the base, hoping to emerge after their doomsday trap had been sprung. An archive capsule of history and messages was shot into orbit, to await retrieval by any future visitors from Earth, and the countdown began. Finding a deserted settlement littered with the corpses of the self-sacrificing colonisers, who had provided cover for the great escapers, the locals amassed in celebration in their tens of thousands, until the rocket's primary reactor exploded and incinerated every living thing on the surface for thirty kilometres in all directions. Tragically, so huge was the explosion, surpassing by far the estimates of the colony's best scientists, that shockwaves heaved and ripped their way through the rock formations within a deadly radius, and crushed or buried alive the doomed escapees.

When Barbaroux's retrieval ship flew over, all that was left of the settlement was radioactive ash, inside a crater of complete destruction. The archives were all that remained to tell the story of what had led up to the explosion, and the rest had been obvious. So complete was the transformation of the landscape that the site could easily have been mistaken for a huge meteorite impact. The grim history was downloaded, and added to the litany of last words from the other colonies.

And so Barbaroux continued to the fourth and final colony. Although furthest away from home, they had chosen well. An uninhabited planet, orbiting second out, but still far enough away to be in a Goldilocks zone, and with a rotating iron core to provide an effective shield against any rogue flares from its sun. A slight tilt to its axis had produced mild seasons, and for years the pioneers had prospered, growing in size rapidly as the frozen embryos were deployed in the quest for viable population numbers for the future. But that was as much history as the archive capsules told of, and there had been no new updates for over five years, and no signs of human life on the surface.

The rescue ship's captain, Ixariah Barbaroux, had expected to encounter challenges and difficulties with all the settlements, but she'd never expected such an apparently total failure for all of them. Her capacious vessel had been big enough to transport any colonisers and their descendants who'd wanted to return. But now it looked like it was vastly over-sized, and would be returning with a complement just a little smaller than when it blasted off some years ago now, with fewer than usual crew attrition rates through natural causes and unforeseen accidents.

Barbaroux had been a teenager when the evacuation rocket missions had been conceived of, to lead their occupants to safer worlds far away from an Earth doomed by an approaching mega-comet. She, and billions more, were expected to stay on the planet and face their fate with stoicism and resolve. Comet AG451 had approached out of a dark zone, and given only a decade's notice of an impending arrival which promised to bludgeon Barbaroux's future into the bedrock.

Ship drives were still in their prototype stage then, but the comet's trajectory allowed for few delays based on health and safety criteria. Soon, the pace and intensity of the previous century's Apollo program were seen again at all the planet's rocket-producing centres. Again and again, trial ships, with new designs of engines capable of the immense voyages that would be necessary, took off on test loops round the Sun. Those that came back were improved upon, and tested further. Eventually, when all-but-one of the next set of prototypes returned from their round trips to Neptune, they were declared the best technology that was likely to be ready in time, and production and assembly of these vessels of last resort became the goal that united humanity at last.

Each populated continent was allowed to nominate a thousand living escapees, with thousands more fertilised and frozen embryos also gathered as the future core of the colony populations, which would be setting up home on the distant planets that were only speculated to exist as habitable. Each continent's rocket then blasted off for the nearest stars in their Armageddon lottery, leaving only a few short years before the predicted impact.

Tragically, after a last unmanned prototype had limped home from the Neptune proving trip, just a month after the coloniser ships had already left, the team of drive engineers realised that their rocket design contained a fatal flaw. As a result, they would run out of fuel and power around half-way through their predicted journeys. There was no way to communicate with or recall them, and so the first batch of rockets would thunder on through space until their drives expired prematurely, leaving them marooned, cocooned and doomed. Every continent felt the despair over the sacrificed lives, but just as regrettable was the wasted countdown time, especially as the comet was now just visible through sizeable telescopes on a clear night.

There was nothing else left to do except scrape together a second batch of fewer, and smaller, rockets in the desperate years remaining. These would be built from revised engine drives that stood a hope of lasting the journeys, and some prototype ship bodies. There were only parts for four this time, and they were all produced at the same facility to save time.

And so it was that the teenage Barbaroux watched the last gasp attempts of humanity to survive the comet's arrival, as they lifted off from the main base within a few hours of each other. Sitting next to her father in her family's accommodation module, she nodded at the screen showing the news updates, and the flames that lit up the sky poured a fiery brightness into the room, which made them both blink. Her father had presumed she had been impressed by the ferocious power that emanated from this last throw of the rocketry dice, but Barbaroux had meant more. She had meant that she wanted to reach out into space too, just like Helena Karlsson, the well-known commander of the last ship, who had been a role model for so many. If, by some miracle, all those left on Earth survived the comet.

Her father agreed when she told him. He knew how determined she had already shown herself to be in surviving the loss of her mother, just a few short years previously. And that resilience was why, many years later, she had progressed through training and commands, and ended up captaining the recovery vessel which would be sent out to rescue the colonies, and offer them the hope of return.

Keeping her crew's morale going, despite the successive disasters, had been challenging. An air of despondency had been inevitable, when at least three out of the four last missions had all failed. There was still hope for the final colony to play with though, at least until the initial contact had proved negative, and the archive capsules had taken on the air of elegiac relics.

The surveyors located the primary settlements readily enough, and the ecolosphere assessors gave the go for entry. This was the first use of the lander ferry, and Barbaroux asked Johnson, one of her most experienced pilots, to fly it. She would lead the expedition, delegating control of the rescue ship to her first officer, Haddad, a former captain himself, who had asked to be transferred to the mission. A landing crew was assembled at the transit dock and the craft readied for launch.

As they broke through the clouds, Barbaroux noticed a strangely familiar landscape of trees and rivers leading to a large lake. She looked around at the monitors showing each wingtip, and saw the wisps spiralling off them. There was some minor turbulence suggesting unstable air, but the sensors had indicated no abnormal pressure systems, and the readings were within the target range. The ship above was keeping a close eye on any atmospheric changes and would inform her of any imminent fronts or storms. Johnson held course.

After approaching the outskirts of the settlement cautiously, they flew over the colony's original landing site, and saw the horizontal outline of the arrival vessel. It had been largely dismantled, leaving much of the framework visible. The external panels had been designed to be reuseable as outer walls for buildings, so it looked like the early years had gone to plan.

There was a clear area to the left of it, so Johnson adjusted the glide angles and lined up the ferry, until eventually the landing motors were needed to bring it down safely, balancing their downwards thrust against the planet's grasping gravity. The arrival went smoothly, kicking up the expected dirt and debris cloud as the last of the thrusters pulsed and let the craft settle gently. The terrain radar had mapped out no abnormalities, and they rested on firm ground.

Within a few seconds, the engines' roar had faded to silence, and the gentle vibration of the airframe ceased. The crew looked at each other in relief. They'd never doubted their pilot's ability, but it was the craft's first deployment and there was always the risk of the unexpected. Barbaroux was pleased with Johnson's flying. They were down safely, and at last the final accounting for any survivors from the fourth colony could begin.

Over the next few hours, scans were run of as many metrics as the craft could measure, and every known combination of bacterial, viral and fungal threat was searched for. Then the AI hypotheticals tests tried to determine any data on unknowables, which also drew a blank. Barbaroux was confident that a perimeter assessment could be authorised, and a small group put on their bright orange protective suits and deployed through the airlock. No immediate threats were found.

Then the captain and her officers suited up and exited, leaving the watch crew, including the pilot, in place in their new temporary base. Everything just one step at a time, and no unnecessary risks. That was why Barbaroux was so respected and liked by her crew. Pereem, the first officer, had been with her through thick and thin since her first command, and harboured no desires of captaincy himself. He preferred to concentrate on working out the options in any given scenario, being exceptionally talented in logistics planning. Having to manage the health, social, and mission concerns of the crew was best left to someone else.

Moving slowly, with each new position surveilled and secured, the landing team progressed carefully through the outer rings of the abandoned settlement. The colonisers' dwellings had been spread out well, within an accessible distance bounded by woodland areas. The trees reminded Barbaroux of the ancient baobabs near her home in the north-west sector of the Southern African Federation.

There were no signs of battle or bloodshed around the deserted accommodation. In fact, there were no clues as to what had happened to their occupants in the last few years at all. Just surface dust, slowly reclaiming the alien buildings that had pock-marked the planet's surface with hopeful settlements.

Doors had been unlocked, suggesting the occupants had not felt threatened, and few had airlocks, indicating the air had been judged safe to breathe normally without filtration. This had been the judgement of Barbaroux's best scientists too, but she took no chances and wanted breathing equipment utilised outside for the first twenty-four hours, pending a longer-term review of samples. With no damage to the buildings, or barricades or trenches, there seemed to have been no final conflict for the colonisers, and their disappearance was still a puzzle. Barbaroux looked around her and called her officers together.

"Okay, first thoughts?" she asked.

"Settlement abandoned for unknown reasons," responded Pereem with a shrug. "No violence or hostilities in evidence. No corpses."

"They must have walked out of here by themselves," suggested Harkeem, a lieutenant who had served with Barbaroux on the previous mission and was happy to follow her anywhere, especially if there was a chance to study evolutionary biology on a distant planet.

"Ground scanning?" Barbaroux asked Tellen, the geology specialist.

"Nothing definitive. No underground tunnels or mines we can find."

"So nowhere for locals to imprison captured colonisers then?" Barbaroux asked the security team leader, Uloko, a formidably-built sergeant from the United States of Central Africa.

"It doesn't look or feel like a prison or a trap to me. We can get the drones out on reconnaissance duties whenever you say. They're all lined up and ready to go."

"Let's do that now," Barbaroux agreed, and a dozen rotored craft set off and headed out on their concentric scouting missions.

Barbaroux, ever cautious, decided to pull everyone back inside to await the new information. After the decontamination routines, they returned to their instruments and scanners to continue their research. Johnson had no new updates from the orbiting ship's sensors, so they were all in a limbo of vigilance, until the reconnaissance updates and video feeds yielded a definitive judgement on the area's security. After a last check of the biodata assessments still showed no threats, Barbaroux allowed requests for helmets off in the main crew area, although protocol dictated that Johnson stayed in isolation just in case.

One by one, the drones came back, after revealing nothing that changed the crew's understanding of what had happened. There were no abnormalities like rival indigenous settlements, mass graveyards or even any places for sacrifices to sun gods. Then the last one returned. It had been unable to uplink and provide a live video feed, so Uloko had to recover the data and forward it to the bridge. Barbaroux gathered the officers, and they started to review it. There was little of note until half-way through. Just over a kilometre from the landing settlement, a small heat signal had been traced to a group of trees, and the drone had piloted itself in for a closer view. Tellen spotted it first.

"There, a shadow by the tree on the right," he pointed out.

They all looked, but it had gone in a few frames. They replayed and magnified, and sure enough, there was a shadow there. It looked like the outline of the upper body of an older woman. The drone had circled round the tree but found nothing further. Pausing the image revealed a shaded hollow on the ground in front of the tree.

"Could be a concealed entrance to a hideaway?" Uloko suggested.

Barbaroux agreed. It was the only thing of note in the data. An exploration team assembled, again led by the captain, and they made steady progress through the landscape that surrounded the settlement. They stopped at regular intervals to assess threat levels, but all seemed calm.

Soon they reached the woods and entered the target area, where the figure of the old woman had been recorded. They spread out to give cover, if need be, and then Barbaroux and Uloko approached the tree that was their objective. Barbaroux called out through her helmet's voice projector several times, then waited, and tried again.

"I am Captain Ixariah Barbaroux from Earth. We're here to rescue colonisers. Is there anyone around?"

She stood back from the tree and waited patiently. She felt sure she could sense someone there. Uloko looked at the infra-red sensor on his weapon and nodded.

"We're just having a look around. If you don't want to come out we'll leave you in peace. You can stay there as long as you want."

She waited a while longer and then turned to Uloko.

"It's time to go," she announced. "We can return tomorrow."

Uloko looked surprised, but turned around and accompanied Barbaroux a few paces away.

There was a rustle in the undergrowth nearer the tree. The visitors turned round, and Uloko readied his weapon. A matted lump emerged from underneath the trunk. The crew sensed the change in atmosphere and formed a defensive circle around the captain instinctively.

The dark mound continued to push itself up, as if the tree's roots were birthing new life. A vaguely human head became apparent, and the visitors gasped. Up to its shoulders it revealed itself, but it was unrecognisable to them as their own kind.

Barbaroux and the others exchanged glances of incredulity, but maintained their defensive positions. The face of the protrusion was criss-crossed with moist green and brown root-like arteries, which seemed to connect it with the tree itself, as though by some unnatural alchemy they had fused together to become a new kind of being.

The head turned from side to side, as if sensing their presence through sound and smell. When it was satisfied, it stayed perfectly still, except for a twitching of its eyelids, as if it was in a deep sleep with vivid dreams. And then its eyes opened. The visitors recoiled in shock. Uloko went into a defensive crouch and avoided eye contact with it.

Barbaroux looked into the eyes in front of her. They had lost the colour in their irises – indeed, any distinction of irises at all, as the sclera had vanished – and it was like looking into two lakes of the blackest green that had been slicked through with oil, leaving only holes in the centres to suggest that the pupils were still functioning.

"Human, yet not at all," Pereem commented through his projector, and Barbaroux gently nodded at the strangeness within the horror. Then the lips parted, and words came forth.

"Still human."

So it could understand and communicate. The mystery moved up several levels in an instant.

"From the colony?" Barbaroux asked.

"Yes," came the second response.

"Female?"

"Yes, as once I was."

"Did you change form by choice?"

"Yes," came the answer, as minimal as it was explosive in its revelation.

Barbaroux looked around her. Her crew were speechless. Several had to look away. There was something primevally repulsive about a face tumoured by strange growths, as if an ancient sailor's devil had been transplanted from a bygone mythology to another planet, and its tentacles replaced by mutated tendrils.

"And the others?" Barbaroux pushed the line of questioning a little further.

"Like me," came the reply, and the crews' hearts sank together at the same instant.

"All?"

"All that survived."

"That explains why we found no other sign of human life," Pereem concluded.

"It's lucky we caught her with the drone," Uloko said with relief.

"Not luck," the being replied.

"You gave yourself away?" Barbaroux quizzed.

"I did."

"But you are part of the tree now?"

"Yes, and it is part of me."

"And the other colonisers?"

"Like me."

"They have all become at one with the trees?" Barbaroux asked again because the answer had been so astonishing. "All colonisers, even the children?" She had to be sure.

"The children could not survive the contamination."

Barbaroux realised the colony's history was even more of a horror story than the appearance of the being in front of her suggested. It sounded tense at reporting the full situation, which was already making the crew's flesh crawl as severely as if they were buried up to their necks in tree roots themselves. There had been thousands of embryos on board her ship, and they should have grown into children by now.

"Contaminated by what?"

"Spores."

Barbaroux swallowed hard. This was no aberrant colony volunteering to integrate with Mother Nature. There had been some kind of biological onslaught, survivable only through some unholy alliance across the kingdoms of life itself. She sent an unspoken, scrambled alert through the keypad on her wrist. Code 157. Suspected deadly sporophyte entities. She knew every step from now on would be much more difficult. And she knew the ferry crew would have received the signal at the same time as the rest of the surveying team. They would all be aware that no one had been consulted about the sending of the code that would change their status forever. And they were also aware of the consequences.

"And the trees," Barbaroux insisted. "Are they a refuge from the infection?"

"They saved us," the being revealed. "They are immune from the fungal threat and could pass that immunity to us when we bonded with them."

The 157 protocol was quite clear for crew exposed to infectious threats at this level. Quarantine. Isolation. If necessary, exile. Their own world had turned upside down, at the moment the being had spoken. The crew felt themselves grimace and stiffen. Some had thought until a short while ago that they would be going home directly. Empty-handed for sure, and the bearers of catastrophically bad news, with every colony having been wiped out with no survivors.

But that hadn't been their fault. And they would have been going home so tantalisingly soon, and after such a long and complex mission. Now, no one knew anything. Except that Barbaroux was making the calls that needed to be made. And the alternative future of bonding with trees occurred to none of them, except as a repulsive recourse. Yet the being in front of them had chosen that path.

Already, work on the ferry had begun, isolating a quarantine area and fumigating the cabins. Already, the rescue ship above had been warned, and its crew were preparing the transit dock for a full biohazard cordon, until the full extent of the threat was revealed. Haddad was looking up the protocol for the transition of authority, in case Barbaroux or Pereem were incapacitated or mortally afflicted. And Barbaroux was already cursing herself.

When the team had returned after the first reconnaissance foray, they had gathered together in the arrival bay for the debrief. They had followed the standard decontamination procedures and only removed their helmets after the analyses had deemed it safe, and Barbaroux had made that call too.

All had breathed the same air except for Johnson, whose role it had been to stay sealed off from the expedition members for at least the first forty-eight hours of any incursion into an unfamiliar territory. One of the best policies ever devised, Barbaroux thought. But there was no time for further pondering. If they were infected, their whole world had changed. It had all happened so quickly. Decisions for the captain. And so she made them and gave her instructions.

"You are all to go back to base immediately," she ordered. "Pereem, assume temporary command of the crew down here as of this moment. I will stay behind for one further hour from now. If I'm not on my way back by then, take off and rendezvous with Haddad and the rescue vessel, and start the return journey as soon as you can."

Pereem felt he should object, but he knew she was right. He'd have done the same thing. Exactly. Like her, he'd have stayed behind to try and get more information from the tree being. But the risk was calculated. It was a unique chance to find out about a form of symbiotic relationship unknown to their science.

His interests in nature and evolution on Earth had attracted him to study the role of mycelium in facilitating communication between trees, through mycelial fungal networks. But there had never been evidence of a leap towards integrating sentient creatures in the model. Until now. So it was no surprise to him that Barbaroux had insisted on staying longer. And how had the trees helped the humans resist the infections? He was desperate to find that out too.

All this passed in several instants. Pereem just nodded to Barbaroux, and she raised her hand and touched him on the shoulder of his suit. She acknowledged everyone with a brief smile, in case it was her last goodbye. The crew were too loyal and experienced to challenge her orders. They all knew what was at stake with her life, and theirs. There was a tension in their bodies at first as they turned to go, which seemed to make movement a little more awkward to begin with, but they started the trek back regardless. They hoped to see the captain again, but none were sure of it.

"You are bold," the being said, when the others had left.

"I am the leader," Barbaroux replied.

"So was I," it responded.

Barbaroux closed her eyes and groaned to herself. She knew straightaway who the being was. So this is what had become of Karlsson. The Helena Karlsson she had watched blasting off into the unknown with her father, and learned much more about in the mission preparation. She remembered the interviews, the tearful goodbyes, the waving as her crew entered the giant escape ship. The best commander in the fleet. Given the last and largest vessel to steer to safety over the last and longest route. Which she clearly had. And now this. Yet all that, for just this?

"You were Helena?" she asked.

"I was, and still am."

"And your ship landed safely?"

"It did."

"How did your mission to colonise become this living experiment in ... hybridisation?" Barbaroux felt more able to ask questions now her crew were a safer distance away, and getting closer to the ferry every moment.

"We were infected by spores we could not detect until it was too late," Karlsson said with a heavy regret. "They lay dormant and then emerged into a contagion that wiped out many of us. We didn't think there was a cure, until one night a severely afflicted coloniser settled himself against a tree trunk to await his death. In the morning, he had been transformed, as you see me now. Very much transformed, but still very much alive. That's when we discovered that, if we became part of them, our damaged cells could regenerate, and the spores could be neutralised. With time for us running out on the surface, we were all confronted with this choice, and we freely took it."

Barbaroux sighed. Karlsson had become so integrated with the tree and its roots that she was almost indistinguishable in places, but what was left of her body seemed to have some limited movement. Her mind had remained relatively intact, it appeared. She could remember all the stages of what had gone wrong.

"What happened to the children?"

"We tried to help them bond with the trees, but their bodies could not survive the process. We helped them as much as we could, but the infections took over. There were severe consequences with unimaginable pain."

"You couldn't have let them die like that?"

"No. They died more quickly as the illness gained momentum. There was no need to carry out mercy killings of them ourselves. The infection produced a madness in the young, like rabies on Earth. They sought water as relief from their terrible thirst, walked into the lake, and drowned themselves. We chose to let them do that, as we could not help them. It was a form of mercy suicide. The spores originated from fungal colonies on the shore there. They were trying to instil a parasitic drive, so they could use us to feed them. Perhaps their voracious appetite explains the lack of native animals here. And with our children too, the parasites succeeded. If we'd landed anywhere else, who knows? The spores might be unique to this lake. How we cursed this choice of location."

Barbaroux felt guilty for sighing with relief inside her helmet. This was an experience as a leader she had never had to go through. It must have been brutal for Karlsson. She could not be judged for it all.

"But some adults survived through the hybridisation process?"

"Yes, many of us did."

"And where are they all now?"

"Look around you."

Barbaroux turned away and gazed at the other trees on the edge of the clearing. From each set of thick, gnarly roots, bedraggled heads had emerged, rising on top of shoulders and protruding like sentient, dishevelled mushrooms. Everywhere she looked she saw them. The trees resembled the baobabs in the savannah of her childhood, but this was not home. This was a form of existing unknown to anyone else apart from the expedition crew and the surviving colonisers, if surviving was what their new existence could be called.

"You do not feel colonised yourselves?"

"We feel saved."

"You are not just subordinate to the trees in every way?"

"Perhaps as with all life, it was the trees that were reaching for consciousness. Through us, they have gained a centre for their sensations, and enhanced awareness of light and sound. And we have gained the possibility of life again. To continue living is not subordination."

"But through you they can see?"

"They could already sense light and shade, and detect some colour differences, like trees on Earth. But we have provided them with the optic nerves that they were incapable of evolving themselves. And centres for the processing of their sensations. Inside our heads."

The rational assessment reminded Barbaroux of the commander the being had once been. Looking at the creature, she had presumed its intellect would have withered away as surely as its surface skin, which had become layered with a soft and malleable bark-like epidermis underneath the slender roots that encompassed it.

"You are connected to the other trees?"

"Yes. We are united by roots and fungal networks, again like trees on Earth. We become coupled with their whole ecosphere."

"And all this because of the crisis caused by the spores, and the infections?"

"Yes."

Barbaroux shook her head again. She felt returning to the ferry after the first reconnaissance had been a disaster and she blamed herself. The whole ferry crew – apart from Johnson – would have breathed in any spores attaching to the suits that had survived the decontamination bay. Karlsson's equipment had not detected them until it was too late, so perhaps their scanners had missed them too.

"The spores will attach to everything, and evade your detection and filtration systems. If you have breathed in the air outside your vessel, or removed your helmets inside it, after returning from outdoors, you will have been infected already."

Barbaroux groaned silently, but couldn't respond at first. Karlsson had been a commander for too long to not grasp what the long pause meant.

"Then you removed your helmets inside your vessel too soon?"

"Yes."

Now Barbaroux felt she was being challenged about her leadership. For the first time in all the years of the mission, she felt like she was a subordinate again.

"It was a bad judgement," she admitted.

"You will be joining us then, if you become infected too?" Karlsson asked.

"I don't know yet," Barbaroux answered, and knew in her heart that actually she didn't know, and anything was possible now.

"You will," insisted Karlsson. "Eventually it may become your only option. It is inevitable if you have been infected, as it is your only way to escape from it."

"And become ... like you?" Barbaroux instantly regretted the note of disdain in her voice.

"We have life. Through the trees we have seen into unknown realms with myriad connections. We can feel the rain through their leaves and sense the sap begin to rise, just as surely as we feel our own blood flow. Through us, and through the trees, this living community has advanced more in a few years than in most of the rest of its history. Through us, the community of life here in these woods can see the sky above in the day. In the night, our eyes reveal the glory of the heavens above it. Who would not want to be part of this adventure, this exploration of what it is to be alive, this affinity across kingdoms, this experiment that could be unique in the universe? And with the benefit of saving our own lives from a cruel and fatal infection? There was no choice for us."

Through this insight Barbaroux, for the first time, felt she was beginning to empathise with and understand Karlsson's transformation, but it was too soon to say what her own strategy would be. It wasn't clear yet whether the spores had already infected her crew. And her. But there were more questions she knew Karlsson needed to ask, and so badly that they came out almost as one.

"But are we the last of our kind? The other colonies? Earth? The comet? Who else has survived? Where exactly are you from?"

Barbaroux looked away. The truth would hurt. But the service Karlsson had given in the past deserved the explanation. She took a deep breath."

"Things did not happen the way you will have imagined them," she began. "The comet did not herald Armageddon. It fractured on entry into icy fragments from around a hollow gaseous core. It did not have the mass we thought it had. Yes, it devastated the western coastline of the Americas with giant tsunamis. But it was not an extinction-level event. The Earth, and humanity, lived on. That was why our rescue ship mission was proposed – to recover the colonisers and prevent any further unnecessary sacrifice."

This time it was Karlsson who groaned. 'And the other colonies?' she insisted.

"All gone. No survivors."

"Then of them all, only we are left, and like this?"

Barbaroux nodded.

Karlsson's eyes closed, and she seemed to withdraw a little into the base of the tree. Barbaroux looked around, feeling the pain of the moment. Now it was evident to Karlsson that all the rest of the voyagers, in the second tranche of ships, had also died in vain. It must have been hard for her to bear. She might have been living with the consolation that the other colony groups could have succeeded. They hadn't, although Earth itself had endured. For years, Karlsson and the surviving colonisers had believed in a reality beyond their adopted planet that was no more than a cruel fiction.

Barbaroux waited. Eventually Karlsson emerged again.

"You are going to join us here then?" she asked, repeating the question from before.

"There have been no decisions yet," Barbaroux answered.

"Then of course you must return to your lander and discuss it with your crew. I wish you well," Karlsson said.

"Indeed so," replied Barbaroux. "Goodbye Commander Karlsson."

"Goodbye Captain Barbaroux."

And with that, Karlsson's head slowly slumped down out of sight. Barbaroux turned and began the walk to the temporary base. She knew the toughest questions waited beyond the airlock. She hurried on her way, updating them on what she had learned as she went. But part of her needed more time, to process all she had heard and learned. She needed to think about the paths that now lay before them. There were going to be no easy decisions, for any of them. The spores had seen to that.

She went through the airlock, and proceeded through the usual sterilisation procedures before finally being greeted by her traumatised crew. Who, this time, were still helmeted, just in case any of them had escaped infection the first time round. She sat down next to them and looked around. Only Johnson was missing, suited up still and safely hermetically sealed away on the isolation bridge with his own air supply.

"I want you all to speak freely," Barbaroux encouraged. "Pereem, what's your assessment of the situation?"

"The risk from the spore contamination is real but unquantifiable as yet," Pereem said. "We don't know how long we've got before we have to choose between fleeing for our lives, or becoming tree zombies or bodies in the lake."

They all smiled at how the situation had been deliberately described with military bluntness and insensitivity, and the tension was broken a little.

"But we do present a high risk to the rest of the crew on the rescue ship," Harkeem added.

"Agreed," Uloko nodded. "We breathed the air here on the ferry without helmets for over an hour, after returning from the first mission, while the drones did their work. We have no idea whether the spores were resistant to our decontamination procedures. Our sterilising gear is probably ahead of what the colonisers had, but the spores might have evolved. As security leader, I should have delayed us removing our helmets."

They could all tell he felt heart-breakingly guilty, and meant every word.

"I am the captain," said Barbaroux with her natural authority. "It's my fault we're in this mess. It's me who needs to say sorry. I approved the action."

"As your second-in-command for years," Pereem responded, addressing Barbaroux directly, "it's always been my job to look after the details. I missed this one, and I take responsibility for it."

"Thank-you," replied Barbaroux, "but the buck stops with me and that's what it'll say in my report."

They all looked at each other, as if to suggest there was nothing more to say about it now.

"Let's look at options then," Barbaroux moved on. "Johnson, have sensors revealed any fungal spores in the air down here yet?"

"None so far that are identifiable," Johnson responded, sounding as perturbed as everyone else about the turn of events. "But there are microscopic entities that we can see. No ID possible on those so far. They could be from edible mushrooms. Or they could be the Grim Reaper's fungal fairy dust. We just can't say as yet."

"Okay," began Barbaroux. "So we can't identify the threat but objectively it exists. How do we run the risks through?"

"We could return to Earth in the quarantined cryabolism chambers," said Oloko. "We must be isolated from the rest of the rescue ship's crew. But we have no information on how long the spores would stay dormant, or what they would do to us during the voyage, if they survived the cryabolism process. Or whether they could break out when we get back to Earth. So

I guess we wouldn't be going anywhere after arrival without years of isolation – probably still in orbit. No one's going to be putting out a welcome mat for us."

"Karlsson reported they had lived here for several years before the spores took hold," said Barbaroux.

"Yes," acknowledged Pereem, "but during that time they were probably evolving their ability to infect human bodies and brains. I'm afraid we can't gamble on much of a dormant period either."

"Well, there we have it," Barbaroux said. "When we get back, we'll have to stay on the rest of the ship, which will become our orbiting quarantine when the rest of the crew have left." She paused as if not wanting to articulate the alternative, but then, with a captain's stoicism, continued. "Or we go back to Karlsson's colony of tree people. And become like them. We don't know how long we'd get, or want, before that happened, but we have to assume it's within a year or so from now."

"Or we cut out the waiting and get on with it. Just find a tree we like the look of and see if we can bond with it!" Pereem joked.

Again smiles. Pereem's humour was welcome. But there was a bizarre ring of truth within it.

"Karlsson informed us that all the trees are part of the community, so perhaps she can play matchmaker," Tellen added.

Pereem grinned at that one.

"So you roll the dice on surviving the return journey and quarantine, or you become a hybrid and merge with another type of life altogether?" asked Johnson. "I'm glad I don't have to make that decision."

They looked around at each other. Johnson indeed seemed fortunate.

"It's going to be an individual choice, of course," said Barbaroux. "And we're going to need some time alone while we think about it. You are all aware of the consequences, either way. I can give you until after breakfast tomorrow, if that seems fair. Then at midday the ferry will have to launch, and the rescue ship can start the journey home. It's not right to delay its departure any further. There were no recoverable colonists, so the main mission has effectively ended. But more importantly, the sooner we get those of you who want to return back in the travel chambers, the better."

They all nodded, and the meeting broke up. They went to their bunks and started to consider the biggest decision of their lives. Few got much sleep, their rest complicated by having to remain suited and helmeted, in the hope of avoiding any predatory spores waiting on the outside of their suits to ambush their hopes of survival. The parasites could be anywhere, everywhere, or nowhere. And as they'd evaded detection so far, it was impossible to say which. There was just the low hum of the air supply pumps to help some fall asleep, like a monotonous and unending mechanical lullaby.

In the morning, they rose, and managed something to eat and drink as best they could in their cabins, although they all disliked using the bypass tubes that allowed them to access sustenance inside their helmets without removing them. Then they reconvened. Most had spent the night thinking about the chances of seeing their home planet again, after the long voyage in which they'd be oblivious to what the spores were doing, if they were doing anything. And then what? They would stay in orbit and receive supplies by logistics drones, until the threat was determined to have passed. Not much of a life, most of them thought, but possibly for the best if both options were bad ones?

Or they could return to Karlsson's tree, and ask what came next. They could become absorbed into a tree and its ecosystem, like the other surviving colonisers. They might live for much longer, the infection being neutralised, and take part in the biggest hybrid species experiment there had ever been, or perhaps ever could be, anywhere. And what if they could still communicate with each other, and with the other colonisers, as appeared to be the case?

"It's got to be your own choice," Barbaroux reminded them, after much discussion. "The quarantine chambers, then orbital limbo until you're declared clear, or living like Karlsson for an unknown number of years down here."

They nodded, appreciative of the directness with which the choice was being framed.

Okolu spoke first.

"My role is to protect the crew. If you all become tree people, there's no one here left to protect. Away from here, there's a chance the spores won't affect us. And we have no positive proof we've been infected – yet."

Barbaroux nodded. She had thought that was what he would choose. Most of the others agreed with him. Then it was Pereem's turn.

"Like all of you, when I heard about the comet my life changed, as I expected everyone around would die. But most of the population didn't. I think I've already had my lucky ticket as a human being. I avoided the comet, and I avoided the fate of the other colonists. But I want to go forward, not back. I want to do something that will advance my knowledge of science. Karlsson has shown that it's possible. I don't want to risk dying in a chamber on the way home. I'm going to stay and join the tree people. Nature has fascinated me since I was a boy. So I'll find a tree to bond with. That's what I'm going to do."

There was surprise on the bridge, but everyone had the same options. It was typical of Pereem that he would choose the one with the most to learn from. And then the captain spoke.

"I'd like to have my say now," she said with a serious tone in her voice, and they all looked at her intently. "I agree with Pereem. Karlsson was right about the symbiosis process. This is a unique chance to evolve the species. I have always had a sense of adventure. And this will be one of the biggest of my life. I'm going to stay here."

There was a sense of dismay amongst the crew that they would be leaving their captain behind, as well as their much-liked first-officer.

"You all know Haddad is an experienced captain. He was a good friend to me in the past too. I trust him to take over. In a few minutes I will contact him on our own channel and talk all this through. So is it just me and Pereem then, staying behind, and the rest of you go back, and gamble your lives together in the chambers and in the isolation to follow?"

The rest of the crew nodded, affirmatively.

After their strained and difficult farewells to the crew, Barbaroux and Pereem made their way back towards the woods. Johnson started pre-flighting the ferry, a process that took around an hour or so. The sooner the crew were in suspended animation, in the chambers in the main ship, the more chance there was of surviving the journey before an infection took hold.

It was a slow walk to the woods. They had been through many crises and adventures together, but they knew this was their final escapade, at least in their current form as a human individual before the hybridisation process would begin. Or so Pereem had thought, until Barbaroux began to speak.

"I need to share something with you, but you are to keep it to yourself. Always," she began.

"I can promise to do that only until I become one of the tree people," Pereem said. "After that, I have no idea of knowing where my thoughts are going to end up, or who the grass will be whispering gossip to."

Barbaroux smiled. It was a reference to an old song from the previous century that they both liked, as they shared an interest in unusual music from the past.

"Pereem," she began again, her tone completely disconcerting him, "you have shown me incredible loyalty, and we have worked together for so many years now I can hardly imagine life without you."

He stopped in his tracks and looked at her face, framed as it was by her helmet and the glow of the mid-morning sun shimmering around the visor.

"But Karlsson shows us the process is survivable - and so do the other colonists," Pereem protested, not quite sure where Barbaroux was going with the line of thinking.

"It's not just the risks of hybridisation out here that are a problem," Barbaroux explained. "I have a genetic disorder from my mother's side. Our last three generations of females have all passed on in middle age."

Pereem was aware of her mother's age when she'd died as they'd talked about it before, along with the effect this had had on Barbaroux as a young woman, left to find her feet in the newly challenging world without her mother. After the comet appeared, her mother had disappeared, as she'd put it, and both events had upended her life.

"What I'm trying to say is, I can't be sure if joining the tree dwellers will extend my life, or shorten it. I don't have all the facts, and I can't have," she continued. "I might just pass on within a year or two anyway, no matter which route I take."

Pereem closed his eyes for a moment. This was something really unexpected for him.

"This was going to be my last mission in any case. I didn't want to tell you, because I didn't want you to feel obliged to come out of loyalty. I didn't want anyone to know. I got my position through hard work and competence, not sympathy."

He knew she was right to have said nothing. The disclosure would have foreclosed her career years ago. But there was more to come.

"We have gotten on so well in the past," Barbaroux continued, "and I feel some additional responsibility for you. I can't accept that you might be left alone all the way out here, so far away from home, and so far from being fully human. Even if you have the colonisers, the trees and the whispering grass for company."

Pereem shook his head slowly, as if this could forestall what he knew was coming. But it couldn't.

"I think you should go back," Barbaroux said.

Pereem looked around him. He had been on the verge of an incredible adventure in evolution, of becoming a part of a hybrid species unknown to science until their landing. It had been worth the sacrifice of his independent humanity, he had thought, especially when the alternative wasn't risk-free either. But now, confronted by Barbaroux's uncertainty over her own lifespan, he was no longer sure of anything. Perhaps his loyalty to her had clouded his reasoning. Perhaps his place was with the others, helping them survive the no doubt long years of isolation in orbit, with only the moon and each other for solace.

"I don't know what to say," he mumbled, far now from his usually confident, decisive self.

"Well, you and Harkeem are two of the best evolutionary biologists out there. You can put that expertise to good use in isolation, and write some research papers, on completely new subjects. The hybridisation process could give vital insights into aspects of astrobiology, and evolutionary adaptation, that we have no knowledge of so far. You just need to take a sample of some symbiotic cells home, and that's the first few years of your return filled up with analysis. You'll have plenty of time to fulfil your dream of being an academic researcher."

"A sample of what, and from where?" Pereem asked, still bemused by the turn of events, which had now turned his life upside down several times in just a few days.

"We'll ask Karlsson," Barbaroux said. "But meanwhile I'll need to contact Johnson and get him to wait for you."

Pereem didn't reply because he couldn't.

"Paul," Barbaroux insisted. "Please do this for yourself, and for me. I couldn't bear to die here, possibly decades before you. It wouldn't be fair."

He nodded slowly and the call was made, and then they resumed their hike to the woods. They soon located Karlsson's tree, and she was waiting for them.

"I thought only you would be staying," Karlsson said to Barbaroux, while raising a gnarled hand towards Pereem.

"You thought right," Barbaroux responded. "But I have a favour to ask, for the pursuit of science."

"I see." Karlsson exhaled slowly. "You want them to return with a sample, so they can work out how the fusing process occurs?"

"Exactly that," Barbaroux responded. "And it may have clues to surviving the infection if the hybridisation also gives immunity."

"I would have asked the same from you."

Karlsson stretched out her arm and lay her hand flat on the ground in front of her, then spread her fingers outwards.

"Take the smallest," she said. "Then wrap it in the moss that grows near the base of the trunk. That will help keep it sterile until you can secure it in your ship."

"I hope you won't miss it too much," Barbaroux said.

"On the contrary," said Karlsson, "I can regrow it. The integration unlocks lots of cellular changes, as you'll find out soon yourself. Your scientists would do well to study them."

"Oh we will," said Pereem. "I can promise you that."

The minor amputation, Pereem noted, released only a small amount of darker-coloured blood from the wound, which seemed to clot itself into a hardened surface surprisingly quickly. The sample was carefully wrapped and secured, and then it was time for the last goodbyes. He thanked Karlsson and wished her well, then looked towards his captain. They wandered over towards the edge of the woods.

"So it's farewell this time then," he said.

"Indeed so, my colleague from another continent."

"You were the best captain I ever served with."

"I was the only captain you ever served with!"

Barbaroux smiled at the humour, Pereem always trying to lighten the load.

"But you'd better not stay too long, or you'll miss your connection."

"Yes, that pretty much sums up my life so far," Pereem replied. "Always in transit to someplace else. Rootless and free, that's me."

"Why not take the chance to do the studies you've always dreamed of?" Barbaroux suggested. "You can get years of research ahead of anyone else on what we discovered, and go on from there. The orbital quarantine won't last forever."

"Possibly, but you're about to go on a journey of discovery yourself," Pereem responded. "It sounds like quite an adventure too. You're going to become part of an organic community, and be connected up through plant fibres and electrical impulses. Yet somehow that's all going to sustain your body and connect with your thoughts. In many ways, I still wish I was staying, so I could go through all that too."

"Well, we're both going to live very different lives from now on."

"I'll think of you on my travels."

"I'll think of you while I'm growing roots. And you'll keep my secret?"

"Whispering grass, don't tell the trees ..."

"Because the trees don't need to know!" Barbaroux smiled as she completed the old lyric.

Despite the comforting reminiscing, the last goodbyes were not easy, but a few hours later as Barbaroux watched the ferry disappearing into the early afternoon sky, she felt at peace. It would not have been fair to suggest that Pereem stayed and shared the life down here with the other colonisers, and with her. She went over to Karlsson.

"Well commander," she began, "I appear to be in need of a guide."

For the first time she thought she detected a smile on Karlsson's face, obscured as much of it was by the sinewy roots and bark-like covering.

"There is a tree waiting for you not far from here," Karlsson said. "The colonist that was due to bond with it didn't make it."

"Didn't make it through the process, or through the infection?" Barbaroux queried, slightly alarmed.

"No, she died of a blood cancer, before the spores could take hold of her. There was nothing we could have done for her."

Barbaroux shivered. That damn illness again.

"Which tree was she going to have?"

"The last one on the edge of the clearing over there," Karlsson said, pointing towards a tree a little further away from the others.

As Barbaroux looked towards it, she felt she could sense it was the right one. It was strangely reminiscent to her of the baobab that had stood guard at her parents' old property in Maun for generations. She remembered hanging old French and Botswanan flags from it as a girl, on their wedding anniversary.

"Thank you Helena."

"I look forward to hearing more about your life when you are part of our community."

"And I of yours," Barbaroux said, as she nodded a last goodbye from her life in wholly human form, and walked towards the lone tree at the edge of the clearing.

As she got nearer, she thought of Karlsson's words, explaining that the colonists had freely chosen to bond with the trees. She had thought that odd at the time, and yet here she was doing exactly the same thing. The alternative was just too grim.

More closely, she seemed to sense a presence around her, even underneath her feet, as if a form of anticipation was building. She paused at the foot of the tree, looking up to take in its immensity. Its huge, bulbous trunk swelled with life, and its branches were bursting out of the top, as if grasping upwards to pull down the sky like a covering blanket.

Laying her hands on the trunk, she felt the roughness of the bark grate gently on her palms. She scanned her eyes across her left hand, over the darker shadows in the skin folds around the knuckles, and then looked across to the right. The merging of everything did not seem unnatural. Not at all.

Slowly, the ground around her feet and the trunk began to gently subside and give way, as if it was granulating through the action of some unseen force. There was a feeling of sinking a little as her weight pressed down above it, but unlike with a malicious quicksand, there was the thought that she could leave at any time. The ground smelled moist, and there was the taste of the fresh earthiness of it all in her throat. Propping herself up on her hands, she lifted herself out of it for a moment and sat on the edge of the new pit below her, and leaned back against the trunk. She looked around her, knowing this would be her last time to experience the woods in her fully human form.

The feeling reminded her of when, on a holiday with her parents, the waters of Mosi-oa-Tunya had thundered past next to them. She'd peered over the edge into the abyss of the plummeting ocean, endlessly falling towards the planet's core. She'd felt a desire to jump in and be both part of it, and lost in it, at the same time. Her mother's hand had prevented her, but she wasn't there now to hold on to her. She hadn't been there for so long. Removing her protective suit and clothing, which she piled neatly by the side of the tree, she drew a last deep breath into her human body and made her peace with what she was about to do.

Then there was a jump with the whole of her life, unreservedly and completely, trading everything for an unknown future of collective being, of symbiosis with a tree and an underground kinship with the other colonists. Her feet impacted with the soil, and then it felt like the soil was parting to allow her to sink more deeply, until her head was level with the brim, and the blue sky domed above her for a last time. After lateral roots spread outwards, like an enclosing web that criss-crossed the space, she was left in darkness. But there was no fear inside her.

Instead, there was an understanding, deeply within, of the giving of herself completely to the force of nature that was the tree, and of the physical coupling with it that was imminent. She could sense a minuscule trembling in the surrounding soil, as the tree began to transform itself into supporting another existence. Tiny tap roots sprang from the heart of the subterranean structure, with fibrous growths stretching out from the nearest to entwine her lower limbs.

There was not a sense of imprisonment or capture; rather, a feeling that they were the harbingers of an act of natural communion, which intensified as the fibres sprouted microscopic hairs that reached in through her skin pores, and plunged into the layers within. The growths spread inside her legs and up through her body, but there was no pain, and the sensations were more of an evolving awareness of parts of her that were normally insensible.

As tap roots wrapped around her spine, and fibrous hairs reached between the vertebrae, there was the thought of becoming tethered not just to the tree but to something more in the soil in which it had taken root. Her mind was dominated by the prospect of the developing symbiosis, and there was no discomfort, only transformation and becoming, as if all her pain sensors had been rewired by a wave of potential.

A soft tingling arose as fibres fastened themselves into her nervous system, and a dull echo quietly thudded through her head, as the crossing of the boundary of the strange unification approached. It was like sensing an increase in humidity in the air as the entrance to a cave got closer. Passing into it, a secondary presence inside her head became steadily more illuminated, with a warm hue that spread from the shadows into the depths, and reflected around the interior of her skull. Stalactites and stalagmites of organic growths extended towards each other from above and below, and then connected with fibrous networks. The correlations deepened and there were echoes of sensations that were not hers.

From a source outside herself, a sense arose of the fluttering of leaves in the calm breeze, and of the faint glow of warm sunlight. Then there was the dull roar of flowing liquid in countless channels, which started way beneath her feet and ended in the tips of the leaves, as if her arms were stretching outwards to the skies, and the noise reminded her of Mosi-oa-Tunya heard from afar. Then it became possible to locate the sources of these impressions, simply by imagining from where they were being sensed. There was an ease of movement from the roots, through the trunk, and on to the outermost edges of the leaves, as though she was once again inside a small mokoro boat, and freely floating in the rivers that transported people and supplies back and forth when the rains came in the Okavango Delta.

Still herself, yet more than herself, there was a linking with nature in a way unimagined before – actual, physical linking – and an increasing awareness of being part of a massive entity that was also breathing in life. Its hold in the soil and the strength of its grasp could be felt, and then there was something else. There was her feeling through it, but then there was also the beginning of it sensing through her. On grasping the nearest roots with her hands, it was as if the tree was experiencing itself from the outside for the first time, and having its very existence confirmed.

Above, the covering layer of lateral roots parted in places, creating pinpricks of light, which grew wider to let in glimpses of the blueness overhead. Slight shivers ran up and down the channels of the tree, as though it was sensing light for the first time, not as a dull comprehension but as something exact, something defined by her sight. The covering above her head then parted completely, and there were clouds forming in the afternoon sky, and again a tremble of exhilaration shimmered even to the uppermost leaves.

Stiffening her legs, and pushing herself upwards, her head emerged from the void, gently propelled from below by the movement of roots and fibrous cords that all seemed interconnected now, and shared her desire to break forth and take in everything around them.

Blinking in the sunlight, her eyes squinted as they adjusted to new ways of seeing, and the newly sinewy skin that covered her face felt the warmth of the rays for the first time. The thought of resembling Karlsson and the others did not unnerve her, for there was a profundity to being at peace with herself. Looking from side to side from the edge of the woods towards the clearing, there was a sense of the tree's own reaction to the revealing of its location and surroundings, as though, relieved from blindness, it was learning how to see.

Turning her head upwards to gaze along the immensity of the trunk to the outstretched branches above, there was the feeling of being at home, for the first time since her mother had died. After all her travels and explorations around Africa, around the globe and then out into space, far beyond any horizon ever imagined when looking out from her bedroom window as a young girl, there was now another place for her. After that night of her return from the hospital without her mother, knowing that the world had forever changed, and there might never be a home again, here was also home now.

Then the cave within her head – with all its corners, troughs and shadowed pathways – beckoned to her, and there was the whole inside of it to explore. Each pathway led somewhere else, through her body and out of it, through the tree and out of it, and then down through the ground and along the fibres that linked her to the nearest tree, and then the next one, and then the next one, and she gasped at the amplification of her very being. Experiences could be shared with other beings in the locality, who could multiply and augment her sensations, until the surrounding environment could be understood as a whole, from without and from within.

Then there was the realisation that time itself had changed for her, and that the sharing of thoughts and sensations might be taking place over many days or weeks, and what had seemed to be instantaneous experiencing and communication could be occurring on a timescale beyond anything she had perceived before.

Consciously navigating the new areas inside her head, there were untravelled routes to be mapped out, as if she was again charting unexplored tributaries of the Okavango as a child. There was the memory of the visit to the Gcwihaba Caves and her staring around, wide-eyed and open-mouthed, at the giant columns percolated from the drips of water within, so many years ago. Holding her mother's hand firmly, there had been the feeling then that everything would be all right, and that they would be able to leave as easily as they had entered.

From her own cave thoughts flowed, through the rivers and channels and out into the roots, and then out into nature itself. There was awareness of what other trees were sensing, of the difference between light and shade, and of the transportation of vitality through their channels. Another image came to the fore, of paddling down the delta streams in her mokoro while following the maps in her head. Then, there was paddling through space, but now, there was also paddling through time, a different time to before the symbiosis.

Slowly, quite imperceptibly at first, other viewpoints floated across her mind, which seemed to merge in the newly open spaces in her head and offer her a way to see the world from outside herself. Shutting her eyes for a moment, the realisation came that connections to the other colonists were forming more clearly now. Heads were slowly appearing up from the spaces below the trunks, where they had also made their peace and their homes, but being the last to do so did not make her feel an outsider.

Growing into this new version of herself now involved other selves, and ways of being, and everything was in all things together, and there were no physical boundaries between trees and selves. But there was not the feeling of drowning in a flood of new sensations and perspectives; rather, there was a sense of enhancement, an evolving understanding of what it was to be both human and more than human.

Looking across at the nearest tree, a head emerged from it and smiled, and within what seemed like just a few moments there was a sense of knowing of who it was, and how they felt, and her own thoughts could be shared back. In what seemed like an instant, her fear of loneliness was lost, which had been disguised as her quest for independence for so many years since the drive back from the hospital. It had caused a void to open up that her father had never been able to fill by himself, although he had tried his best. The aching emptiness in her chest, which at times had seemed to darkly absorb all her positive thoughts and leave her stranded on an opposite shore from her emotions, need never be felt again.

More and more colonisers then intertwined and became part of her world. Soon there was the feeling that her consciousness could move, as if floating back and forward from the cave of innumerable couplings inside her head, through the streaming fibrous synapses that now stretched underground and reached upwards through trees and colonisers alike.

Like an expanding cloud in the sky above reaching out to combine with and envelop others, the networks continued to grow and join with other hubs of experiencing and understanding and sharing, until there was a sense of being part of a colony in a giant nest, where the survival of the whole depended on the health of all the beings that enabled it. And then an association came through that she recognised most of all, and the commander was with her again.

They shared their relief that the symbiosis had gone so well. It was clear now why there had been no resistance to adopting this new way of existing, and why the surviving colonists had opted for it in their entirety. After much exchange of ideas and sensations, over an unknowable period of time, her withdrawal from the cave in her mind was effortless, as if a membrane could be traversed just by imagining it.

Then there was a different recognition. Hers wasn't the only cave now in her mind. There was another presence that could be sensed, which was deepening its connection with her, and sharing the vast, fibrous lattice that now entwined them both. Moving back inside her own cave revealed that a tunnel had formed in one of its corners. Moving towards it, there was a strange warmth emanating from it, and then the revelation of what it was.

The tree that was her host, and which might yet save her life twice over, had consolidated their symbiosis and established its own centre in her head. All its previously separate perceptions and needs and reactions could now have a focus through the sharing of a part of her mind. And so they would help each other. It was a new form of existence for both of them. There was an excitement of possibilities that rippled outwards to the tips of her fingers and back, and then out to the tips of the leaves and back, like pulses of benevolent energy. Withdrawing from the tunnel and pulling back from the cave allowed her to catch her breath, and have her own space to contemplate these curiously intoxicating new worlds.

In this interior space, her thoughts were hers again, and belonged only to her. She did not have to tell the trees, or her tree, or anyone else, anything if she chose not to. She could be alone in her new home, or part of the community, as she wished. She was safe from the infection, as were the others. Whether she was also safe from the condition that had robbed her of her mother, and of the grandmother she had never met, only time would tell, but the regenerative aspects of the symbiosis gave her a hope she'd never had before. The loss of her mother had taken away her childhood in the past; but in this most extraordinary way, she had taken back her best chance of a future.

Daughtermother

I know you will blame me. You will think me heartless and an unworthy daughtermother. You will want to ask why I didn't offer myself instead.

You were not there. You did not face my choice. I would have given up all the shelters in all the woods in the world, and all the fires that glow in the night, to have had another choice. But I did not.

I am going to tell you why I had to do it. This is my story, but it is also yours.

There was a struggle in the night. We were sleeping under a bitter bark tree to shelter from the night rain, and daughterfather had lain broken branches against the trunk to cover us further. I heard a breaking of twigs nearby and pressed sharply at first on daughterfather's shoulder, then much harder, then pinched him in the last grip with my nails. He awoke and understood immediately. The three touches had meant danger, very close, very soon. He picked up the rock he always kept next to his right foot, and crawled quickly out of the shelter, but the enemy was too close.

I heard the noises of struggle as I moved out from under the branches, and then daughterfather yelled in agony, as the

enemy pierced him with a sharpened stick that came blood-
ied out of his back. But daughterfather hugged him closer
still, knowing I would have his vengeance, and I did, bringing my own rock down on Enemy's head with a hateful crack
that echoed through the forest. Again and again I struck,
and Enemy slumped against daughterfather's proud being,
until he was cast off. Enemy would never have access to my
body or my daughter, and as he lay dead on the ground I
kicked out with contempt.

Daughterfather looked down at his wound and knew he
was done. I made to slowly withdraw the stick, but his eyes
rolled up in their face holes and caught the light of the half
moon above. I lowered him to the ground and raged inside,
but stayed silent as the flames built inside my chest. Then
I snapped, and smashed my rock into Enemy's skull until
there was nothing left but mush and fragments of bone.

Our lives had changed, and we were on a different path
now, without daughterfather to protect us. I removed the
stick carefully from him as though he could still feel the
pain, and then dragged his body down to the lake. I nuzzled
our noses one last time, and then pushed daughterfather
away from me into the waters. Then I washed his blood from
my arms. The night was still. My heart was not.

I left Enemy's body to be devoured by the creatures of
the forest, and went back to the shelter of branches. While
stroking daughter's hair in the night to keep her asleep, I bit
on a tree root to keep my sorrow inside. In the morning, I
told her that daughterfather was away hunting, and that he
would return after the cold times.

We survived for many moons, and daughter learned to walk
more upright, and more confidently. I caught fish with my
hands and ripped their skin off with my teeth. Then I chewed

through the flesh, removing the bones, and passed the lumps of moistened food to daughter, who devoured them gladly.

We kept out of the sight of other childfathers, who would take me and kill daughter. I knew the sickness in their hearts before the giving of life came, and I did not want another child. Each night we slept under branches with rocks and sticks to hand. I kept the stick that had killed daughterfather. In his memory it would kill again if we were in danger.

I taught daughter to not step on dry leaves and twigs, so she could move more quietly through the woods. I showed her how to make stone funnels in small rivers, to trap fish in the shallows. She found out how to bury her waste so we could not be hunted, and where best to drink pooled water after the rain. Slowly, she learned her way around the area of the woods we lived in, and began to leave her own secret markings to show food nearby.

One day, she picked up a small shell and offered it to me. It was my first gift from her. I smiled and kissed her head, and she smiled back. I put it inside the fur I wore, in which I'd cut a small pouch to keep things. There was a warmth in our stomachs when we were close together that day. She knew I would always look after her. She was wrong.

Other fathergroups travelled through our area of the forest, but did not stay many days. We had hidden the food shrubs behind old branches, and even coloured the barkfruit with bright berry juice so they would not risk eating it. We kept out of sight, with our handfuls of dried fish to chew on, and our berries, carried on curved bark pieces. At night, daughter would sleep in my arms to keep us both warm, and I would pull my furs around us as we settled down. When I couldn't sleep, I felt around for worms and insects, and bit them in half quietly, so I could share them with daughter when the first sun rose.

But our peace was not to last. Over the next few days, I felt that we were being watched from far away, but not by others like us. There were many animals that hunted us, as we hunted and killed them. We were all just meat for each other. I made sure daughter only played where I could see her, but deep inside I felt our lives were soon to change again.

And then one day I saw it. It had come a little closer this time, and did not care if I knew it was there. It was sure of how things would end, as it was too big for me to take down on my own. Although ageing, it was still a clawtooth, with huge front teeth that could bite cleanly through the throats of much bigger animals than me.

Too slow to hunt with a pack, it had probably been cast off to hunt by itself, and end its days with a slow, lonely death. Only it did not die soon enough. And it was hunting us now. It kept its distance, watching us for weakness, and becoming surer we were on our own. Even daughterfather would not have fought it. He would have lured it into a trap, by digging a pit with spikes in it. But I could not look after daughter and do that. We had to keep moving, hoping that Clawtooth would choose easier prey. But it kept following. I could see it did not move like the others of its kind. It might have had the sorebones.

I was left with taking a chance. I would cross the shallow part of the lake at night, when both suns had long gone down behind the hills, and it would lose our smell. It would be stranded on this shore at daybreak, and we would be across the other side. There were fewer trees but many bushes, and we would adapt and move on, until daughter was older and stronger, and we could return to the woods, where if Clawtooth still lived we would trap him together, and eat well for many moons on his flesh.

I waited until it grew dark and watched as the clouds came in from the mountains, spreading themselves out above the lake, and hiding us from the moonlight. It was time to take our only chance. I took daughter in my arms and carried my stick through a hole in the fur I wore, which daughterfather had long ago scraped from an animal's body for me, with a sharp stone.

The water washed cold over my ankles, but did not slow me down. I hurried to take advantage of the clouds above, for I did not know what might be waiting across the shore. I trod swiftly, but tried to keep down the noise of the splashing around my ankles, as each foot left and re-entered the water. From time to time, I switched daughter between arms, but also let her walk where the water was just over my feet. This helped rest my aching shoulders, and I knew that like this we could make it.

I looked up at the skies above the hills and saw many lights shining through the darkness. The cloud cover was breaking, and I would have to hurry. I picked daughter up, and we made the shoreline just as the clouds parted over us and moon-light streamed down. There were many bushes ahead, and we sneaked into the middle of one and went to sleep, as we were both exhausted. It would be a new day soon and we could start again.

The darkness of sleep in my head gave way to the light outside from the first sun, and I blinked and rubbed my eyes. Then I opened them to see daughter sleeping soundly, still at my side. I knew the dangers of sudden movement in strange places, so took care to lift my head slowly to see through empty spaces in the bush cover. I could see no danger, so closed my eyes again and listened, as if forcing my ears to extend like snakes along the ground in all directions. And then I heard it. A low grumbling noise. My heart sank. Without needing to look, I knew what it was. My plan had failed. Clawtooth was not far. He had not followed us across the lake. But he had circled round the shore during the night, and he had found us.

I opened my eyes again and looked slowly over towards the grumbling noise, forcing myself to have the courage to see what I knew would be there. And he was there, lying on the ground, facing where we had entered. If he came in after us, I had my stick. It would hurt him, but I knew he would be too strong. He could also just wait, and not risk getting injured. He did not have to. I had almost no berries left, as I had not been able to carry daughter, as well as food, across the water. I looked around me but did not see edible leaves or insects. The trunks of the bushes were too small for barkfruit. I dug with my hands into the soil but found no grubs. Before daughter stirred, I held her close and wept, so she would not see my tears.

During the day, I gave daughter the last of the berries, but I knew she was still hungry. I did not care about my own hunger. There was going to be much worse to think about. I cursed Enemy. He was responsible for all this. Daughterfather and me could have killed Clawtooth. I tried in my head to think of what else to do, but I knew there was only one way out. And it tore at my heart to think of it, as if Clawtooth had already bitten through it. I kissed daughter's head. It helped that she was tired out after the night before, and slept most of the day. As the first sun dropped down over the edge of the world, I knew our time together was almost eaten up. When the second sun also lowered itself down, the last clouds above us glowed with fear.

When it was dark, we got up and made our way out of the bush. Clawtooth was still there, waiting in the cold moonlight. He did not move. He just watched us, as if he knew what choice I had made. I hugged daughter and told her to sit down. She was wild-eyed with fear, for she had seen Clawtooth too. I held her hands and squeezed them tight one last time. Then I turned away and walked back towards the lake. Clawtooth did not follow me. I shut off my ears with my hands and walked alone into the lake, the moonlight spreading my shame across the waters. I did not look back.

Reaching the other side, I recognised the way we had come, and made my way carefully back towards the forest. One of our old shelters was not far, and I made my way to it. I had a sleep of tears, which was not really sleep. In the middle of the night, when I was most awake, I took out the shell daughter had given me, scooped out a hole in the earth nearby with my shaking fingers, gave the shell one last kiss, and then dropped it into the hole. Then I covered it over.

In the morning, I fed on the berries and barkfruit I knew grew close, and collected many more on a strip of bark. After that, I stood up and listened for the sounds of any fathergroups in the area. Very distantly, towards a clearing, there were some noises of branches being broken. A fathergroup was probably setting up a new shelter. I headed towards them.

As I approached, a boy with a small stick in his hand saw me and ran to the others, tugging at their hands and pointing. I had been seen, and kept on walking. I was no threat to them, but they might have enough childmothers in their group already, and not want any more.

I moved towards them, my eyes looking to the ground ahead, showing them I was not a danger, because I could not see who was strong or weak. There was nothing else for me now. If I was accepted, I would have to join with another childfather and try to start life again. I walked towards the fathergroup with my hands full of the barkfruit and berries. Other childmothers watched, as I walked past and towards the leaderfather. He looked at me, looked at my offering, and then reached for his sharpened stick. He got up and walked towards me. He poked around the food in my hands and stuck his stick into a moist piece of barkfruit, and, taking it carefully to his mouth, bit into the flesh. He chewed it over and over, as if my worth to him could be measured by its taste. Then he nodded.

I let out my aching breath. I was to be accepted. I would have another child who would have a child who would have a child, and so it would go on. And one day, after many, many moons, a child of my branch might understand that, for life to have reached them, many hard choices had to be made.

Printed in Great Britain
by Amazon